GIFT OF THE GOLDEN PEARL

GIFT OF THE GOLDEN PEARL

MICHAEL XAVIER BOGGINS

Gift of the Golden Pearl

For information about this title or to order other books and/or electronic media, contact the publisher:

Michael Xavier Boggins
michaelxavierboggins.com
mboggins@cox.net

ISBNs:
978-1-7341480-2-2 (softcover)
978-1-7341480-3-9 (eBook)

Printed in the United States of America

Cover and interior design: 1106 Design

*To my daughters Sarah and Abby for their
many recommendations and encouragement*

*To my sis Rebecca for her many
editing efforts and support*

*To the awesome team at 1106 Design
for shepherding me through the publishing
process for a second time*

*And last, but not least,
thanks to the author of all things*

CHAPTER ONE

JENNY'S FAMILY TRAVELED to the beach every summer—it was a tradition. As far back as Jenny's memory carried her, she could feel foamy surf, sunbaked sand, and a ceaseless but pleasant breeze.

An only child, she was permitted to invite a friend or two, but, this time, neither of her closest companions could join her. She loved her parents, but, at fourteen, she wished Ashley and Danyelle were walking the shore with her. The three had met at summer camp when they were eight years old. Like Jenny, neither Ashley nor Danyelle had siblings. Both had arrived at camp—their first year attending—having had no older brothers or sisters to pave the way. Perhaps the counselors' decision to group them for a challenge activity was deliberate, or perhaps it was fate, but, in either case, it cemented their friendships. They attended the same school, but, until they met each other at summer camp, they didn't realize they lived in the same sprawling neighborhood.

Each of the girls navigated life from different perspectives. Jenny, fair skinned, with silky chestnut hair, was a rule follower who preferred to avoid risk. Danyelle's creamy dark complexion matched her curly black mane; she was a feeling type who connected emotionally. Ashley, a true blonde who took on a golden tint in the summer months, liked an adrenaline rush and was the daredevil of the group. Their differing personalities made for an odd balance, and, though they teased and tested each other, if one or more of them were threatened, they would ban together to fight a foe—boy or girl, canine or feline, geek or athlete.

Jenny considered the week ahead as she walked and, without realizing it, had traveled two-thirds of a mile from the light-gray, cedar-clad cottage her parents had rented. She turned to start back but, instead, decided to wade into the greenish-blue water. The late afternoon sun glimmered on the surface and brought out the red in her hair. As the waves slapped against her knees and the sand eroded beneath her feet, she again contemplated the coming week and struggled to improve her outlook. A sudden gust blew a wispy lock into her right eye, which smarted as if a misguided insect had stung her. Jenny looked downward and began to rub away the irritation when a quiet voice blended with the roar in her ears and said, "Hello."

She looked to and fro but saw no one close by. When she stepped toward land to gain firmer footing, the little voice spoke again: "Hello." Jenny covered one ear to eliminate half the background noise, and a third "Hello" emanated from somewhere; she didn't know where, but, being a polite, well-raised girl, she responded in kind, "Hello." There was no immediate reply. Her father had told her tales of seamen who heard voices, and, so, she dismissed the voice as a trick of wind and wave.

"Hello." Jenny heard the word again, floating in the freshening breeze.

"Where are you?" Jenny asked, grasping to understand.

"Look downward," the voice said in a gentle tone.

"I see only water," Jenny said as she scanned the sandy bottom.

"I'm just below the sand by your right toe."

Jenny jerked her foot away and nearly fell in the salty wash.

"Don't worry. I won't cause you any harm."

Jenny knelt in the cool, rushing surf, trying to improve her perspective, but the tide was rising, and, with each successive wave, she dug her hands into the sandy bottom, straining to stay upright.

"Can you see me now? A wave has uncovered part of me."

Jenny plunged her hand into the motionless wash and dragged her fingertips through the shifting sands, stopping when her little finger brushed a crusty shell.

"That's me."

She struggled to pull the partially buried oyster to the surface, as the choppy sea threw salty water upward, threatening her squinted eyes. When Jenny freed the creature and cleaned away the remaining sand, she could see the oyster was a large old specimen.

Feeling foolish for believing, she spoke aloud, "Have you been speaking to me?"

"Yes."

"I could be wrong, but I don't think oysters normally speak," Jenny said in jest, still doubting her senses.

"I'm not speaking like you do, but my way allows you to understand what I'm saying in your mind."

"If you say so, but why are you speaking—I mean *communicating*—at all?" Jenny asked, looking around to make sure no one had come near.

"Because there is something important that I need to give you, if you want it."

"Important?" Jenny questioned.

"Yes, life-changing."

"You mean an actual thing?"

"Yes, a thing—a special thing. The pearl that lies within my shell."

"A pearl?"

"Yes, a golden pearl that has a unique power."

"'A unique power'?"

"Yes. As long as you possess the pearl, you'll be able to answer one question for anyone who asks."

"A question? Like, 'What's for dinner?'" Jenny asked with a smile.

"Any question, but most would ask something of greater magnitude—such as, 'How long will I live?'" the oyster continued. "Be warned, however; once you are asked, you will be compelled to answer, even if what you say is difficult to hear for the one who posed the question."

"I don't know—that sounds really scary," Jenny said, after considering what the mollusk had said.

"In a way, it is. Like any significant gift, the bearer does carry a weight. But answering important questions can also change lives, save lives, protect, and give joy."

"Maybe you should be speaking to someone else. I'm only fourteen," she said, quietly weighing how intense it all sounded.

The oyster continued, gently but firmly, "Two things further: You cannot use this power to answer your own question, and, if given away, the pearl can never be yours again . . . . Do you want my pearl, daughter?"

"Daughter?" Jenny asked with surprise.

"Just an expression."

Jenny grew quiet for what seemed a long time before answering, "Yes . . . I think I do."

"Are you certain, my child?"

"It sounds like a big responsibility, but I still want it," Jenny answered, fighting against her risk-averse instinct. "Wait—won't it hurt you?" Jenny asked, looking at his tightly closed shell.

"Just a pinch," he answered and then said softly but without fear, "It will be my last act in this world."

"'Last act'?" Jenny asked, but, in truth, she suspected what he meant.

"Yes. I shall die once I give you my gift."

"I don't want it, then. I'm not going to be the one to kill you," Jenny answered loudly.

"Understand, child. My journey is at an end either way . . . I am old, and it's my time."

Perhaps it was her depressed mood or that he seemed such a kind being or a measure of both, but the thought of his death filled her eyes with tears that welled beyond their boundaries, sending droplets down her cheeks.

"No need to cry, daughter. We all must move to the other side when the part we've played is finished."

"I'm sorry," was all Jenny could muster.

"I knew your heart when you neared. It is a good heart. You should always follow it."

Those were his last words, and with them still echoing in the wind, his shell opened, revealing an orb so perfect, so intense an iridescent gold, that it had the effect of taking one's breath away. She carefully lifted it and held it tightly.

Jenny walked back to the great sandy beach, looking each way, ensuring no one was nearby. With bare hands, she dug a deep hole at the edge of a dune; after laying her friend carefully at the hole's bottom, she covered him and marked his grave with a shell.

She stood and slowly walked in the direction of the beach house, holding her precious possession.

CHAPTER TWO

VACATION MEMORIES GAVE WAY to the rhythms of everyday life, especially this year, as Jenny nervously readied for her first year of high school. She had hidden the mysterious gift in the base of the musical jewelry box she'd received on her seventh birthday. At night, she would occasionally raise the lid and remove the delicate handkerchief that she'd carefully folded around her gift. Each time she looked at the pearl, it reminded her of that remarkable summer day. And as the music box would wind down, the magical tinkling of "Swan Theme" filled her room, which ideally set the mood as she rolled the beautiful gold sphere in her cupped palm. When the box's mechanism could no longer manage another note, she carefully stored the pearl and turned the box's key, so that it would be ever ready when it was time to look again.

Though she thought of her treasure from time to time, the bedtime visits became less frequent, given the emotional and scholastic demands she now faced. Then, a fateful day brought the pearl's promise to the fore. When standing at her locker at the school day's beginning, Danyelle arrived—visibly upset—almost frantic.

"What's wrong?" Jenny could tell she'd been crying.

"My dad is talking about moving."

"Moving . . . moving where?"

"Like a million miles away to the middle of nowhere."

"Where?"

"Oklahoma or Nebraska . . . somewhere . . . somewhere away from here, and you and Ashley. This can't happen." Danyelle's voice was steeped in anger.

Jenny reached out and held Danyelle's arm. "Is this for sure?"

"I don't know. He told mom he has a few days to decide. It's for his stupid job. I mean, I know his job isn't stupid, but . . . you know what I mean. He sounded like he wasn't sure. Like it was good for his career or something."

"Maybe he'll tell them 'No.'"

Danyelle grew quiet for a moment and put her head down, leaning backward until the lockers stopped her motion. "I wish I knew how to show him this isn't good for us . . . that's all."

"Does Ashley know?"

"Not yet. I was looking for her . . . we're going to be late . . . hurry," Danyelle blurted out when she glanced at the clock.

As they raced to class, Jenny thought about the decision Danyelle's father faced and how life would change if Danyelle was gone.

That evening was full of rapid-fire texts as the trio shared feelings of fear, denial, and sadness, and, all the while, Jenny kept her secret. She wanted to believe that it held the key to their predicament, but she didn't know how to broach a subject that even her lifelong friends might find way too crazy.

CHAPTER THREE

JENNY SLEPT ANXIOUSLY. Her night was fraught with nightmares of her friends in need of rescue from numerous attackers, but, no matter how far she stretched her hand to help, her reach was inadequate. She woke up feeling like she hadn't slept at all. She swung her legs over the side of her bed, shuffled to her jewelry box, and pulled out the pearl. She held it in her hand and let her mind find that sunny day when she'd heard that small voice. At times, she doubted that it had happened at all, as if it were a dream or fantasy, but the pearl she held said different. At that moment, she decided that, when they sat down for lunch, she would tell Ashley and Danyelle the story of beach, oyster, and pearl.

Jenny felt her heart begin to race as she approached the table at which Ashley and Danyelle were sitting. Her arms, normally strong and steady, felt rubbery and weak. *They're your forever friends, your spirit sisters—they will understand,* Jenny told herself, yet her resolve to tell her story was fading. *Tell them!* Jenny scolded herself, fed up with her apprehension.

"So, there's something I need to tell you . . . something that happened at the beach," Jenny began before pulling out the chair opposite her friends.

"I don't really feel like talking about the beach. It's going to make it worse—like we're never going to be together again," Danyelle responded as Ashley nodded.

"This is different. I'm sort of scared to tell you," Jenny said in a tentative tone.

"Is it about a boy?" Ashley whispered.

"*No*—sorry, *no*—not a boy. It might be something that can help—I mean *help Danyelle*."

"Wait. How could anything that happened at the beach change what's happening with Danyelle?" Ashley asked, confused.

"I know it doesn't make sense, but maybe . . . I need to explain, but it isn't easy to talk about."

"I don't get it, either, but now I'm all ears. So, what, pray, tell, does the beach have to do with my dad taking that job?" Danyelle said, moving her chair closer to the table.

"What's with the 'pray, tell'?" Ashley laughed.

"Shut up. I read it in English class. Don't change the subject. Come on, Jenny—talk."

"Okay. I was walking down the beach, wishing you were with me and thinking the week was going to be kind of boring when I heard . . ." Jenny continued telling the tale from start to finish, ending with a question, "So I'm crazy—right?"

At first, neither of them said a thing, until Ashley finally spoke. "Jenny, are you sure you didn't fall and hit your head on an oyster?"

"*Ha, ha.*" Jenny made no attempt to hide her sarcasm. "I guess I'd say the same thing if you told me an oyster talked to you at the beach. The more I say it, the stupider it sounds. But I have the pearl. What would you do? Who would you tell? I should have kept it to myself."

"Sorry, but a talking oyster? Too bad it wasn't about a boy," Ashley giggled, trying to lighten her approach. "Danyelle?"

"I'm trying to picture this oyster. I mean, did it have a tiny little mouth or something?" Danyelle asked, trying earnestly to understand.

"No, it didn't have a tiny little mouth. It somehow made me hear his voice in my head," Jenny answered, covering her face with both hands.

"In your head?" Danyelle asked, not really expecting a response.

"Yes, in my head," Jenny answered.

"You have always been the responsible one," Ashley replied. "A talking oyster sounds like something that would happen to me, not you."

"Look, if you say it happened and that a gold pearl can tell us what to do, I want to try it. I mean, if nothing happens when we try, we're no worse off. Why not?" Danyelle said after a short silence.

"I go through these times feeling like it never happened. Just last night, I started thinking I'd imagined all of it, but when I look at the pearl, it brings it back. I can feel the water and his crusty gray shell—it's got to be true," Jenny said, hoping she could further convince her friends and shed her lingering doubt.

"Let's try it tonight. I want to see this pearl," Ashley said, slapping her hand on the table.

"Really?" Jenny answered, surprised.

"I'm down for the pearl," Danyelle laughed.

It was Friday, and Jenny knew her mom would be good with a sleepover. It wasn't a complicated plan: rendezvous at Jenny's house to see the oyster's gift, and, more importantly, to determine if it held the power Jenny had described.

CHAPTER FOUR

DANYELLE'S MOTHER PICKED UP ASHLEY en route to Jenny's. Their back-seat whispers were of Jenny and how to support her, given that neither Danyelle nor Ashley believed any pearl, no matter how magnificent, could answer questions. They knew *something* had happened on that beach, but, whatever it was, they feared Jenny had had some type of breakdown, birthed out of teenage loneliness. This was so out of character for Jenny—the rule-following, logical, responsible Jenny.

Danyelle and Ashley waved goodbye to Danyelle's mom as they climbed the stairs to Jenny's front door. "We're on her side—no matter what," Danyelle said to Ashley.

"No matter what," Ashley agreed as she slowly reached for the doorbell.

Jenny greeted them at the door, helping Danyelle with her backpack. "Sorry, I didn't hear you drive up. I had my cycling playlist turned up pretty loud. I'm nervous about tonight. I know you guys don't believe everything I told you . . . I can feel it. It's okay, I get it."

"It's just . . . " Danyelle started to explain when Jenny's mom interrupted.

"What's up with you three tonight? You're so serious. It's a sleepover. How about a few smiles?" Jenny's mother asked, trying to improve the mood. "My treat . . . what do you want on your pizza?"

"Sure, mom. I think cheese is good—and thanks," Jenny halfheartedly answered as they started to climb the stairs to her room.

"Only cheese?" Jenny's mom called from the kitchen, still befuddled by the girls' attitudes.

"Yeah, cheese is fine," Jenny yelled back before shutting the door to her room.

"Did you get the candles?" Ashley asked.

"No—mom wouldn't let me," Jenny answered disappointedly.

"That sucks. Wait—did she think we would torch the place?" Ashley asked, cutting to the chase.

"Of course! She doesn't trust me," Jenny answered in frustration. "She said we could use these," Jenny said as she plugged in an extension cord and turned off the desk lamp. A dim blue-violet glow illuminated the room. "They're the lanterns we hang during Halloween."

"I always thought those lanterns looked more like some Christmas thing than Halloween—I mean, sort of," Ashley said, initially hoping for a little giggle.

Danyelle pulled out an incense burner. "I like them, and I think they're a little spooky. It'll get us in the mood."

"There *are* Christmas ghost stories," Ashley smiled.

"The oyster guy didn't say anything about candles or incense, but I'm down for anything that will help," Jenny said as Danyelle and Ashley exchanged glances.

When they'd finished their pizza, they again turned off all the room lights and illuminated the lanterns. Danyelle lit a cone, and a pleasant-smelling haze slowly descended upon the lanterns, whose light cast off eerie, shifting specters.

They sat in a circle, legs crossed, as if preparing for a seance. Jenny held the pearl in her hand so that all could see it, as if to say, *See—I know you don't really believe me, but it's real.*

"Danyelle, if you still want to do this, I will close my hand, and you can ask what you want to know," Jenny said with false confidence, trying to sound like she'd done this many times. "Wait," Jenny said as she set the smooth golden object at her feet. "Let's talk about the question. You only get one—I mean one for *forever,* so it has to be like the most important thing *ever* to you."

"What else could ever be more important? I may never see you guys again if we move, or at least for a long time," Danyelle answered.

"If you're sure," Jenny responded. "So, what do you want to ask?"

"Well, maybe . . . How do we keep from moving?" Danyelle suggested.

"I don't like it. It could answer *Kill your dad* or something, and that won't do any good. Assuming you won't poison him," Ashley joked. "I think it should be totally specific.

Like . . . If my dad accepts the job, will it be good for my family and me?"

"Ashley's right. I mean *she's crazy*, but she's right. You could ask your one question and get nothing out of it," Jenny conceded.

Danyelle nodded, "Do you think the pearl is going to actually speak or something?"

"I don't know," Jenny answered. Then she stood, opened her door, and looked down the hall. "All's clear." The sense of apprehension was palpable, but there was also a sense of excitement, like a first date, when all seems new. Jenny sat back down and took the pearl in hand. "I guess I'm ready, if you are."

Ashley whispered the question again in Danyelle's ear and then added that it was worth a try—for Jenny's sake if nothing else.

"Okay, so my question is: If my dad accepts the job, will it be good for my family and me?" Danyelle asked in a slow, deliberate fashion.

Initially, the only exception to the room's silence was Jenny's heartbeat, pounding in her ears. The girls' eyes darted from side to side. Suddenly, the smoke that was hanging in the air swirled like a dust devil in a backstreet corner. Jenny began to feel dizzy, almost nauseous. She lowered her head and closed her eyes, hoping to restore her senses, but it provided no relief. She felt as if she were going to faint. Then Ashley and Danyelle watched as Jenny raised her head and opened her eyes. "The manufacturing facility your father will manage will close within a year after his arrival. John Henderson knows this, but he is also jealous and knows your father's abilities exceed his own—he feels vulnerable. Henderson is manipulating the situation in hopes that your father will accept the position so he will no longer be a threat. There will be no position for your father once the facility closes. If your father accepts the offer, difficult times lie ahead for you, your father, and your family," Jenny said, in an all-knowing voice that sounded like she'd advanced fifty years forward in age.

When the last word left Jenny's mouth, she came to—as if awakening from a trance. She looked at her friends. "I started feeling weird. I must have blanked out for a second. I thought I heard waves, like I was back at the beach. So, I guess nothing happened?"

Ashley and Danyelle stared in disbelief.

"*Nothing happened*! I thought your head was going to start spinning around. Are you okay? You scared the shit out of me. Sorry about the French, but you did," Danyelle panted.

"That was . . . I don't know what that was," is all Ashley could manage.

"What are you talking about? What happened?" Jenny asked, trying to understand.

"I don't know what happened. You started talking about my dad and the job. It was all bad, by the way. I was messing with you about your head spinning around, but it was like you drifted to somewhere else while you answered the question. You didn't sound mean or anything—just different, like you were older or something," Danyelle explained.

"To me, it was like you were hypnotized or something," Ashley added, still amazed at what she had seen and heard.

"Yeah, it was like you were hypnotized—like they show in the movies. Good one, Ash."

"Can you hand me a sheet of paper and a pen?" Danyelle's heart was pounding. "I need to write down what you said . . . if dad accepts that job, we're doomed . . . my whole family."

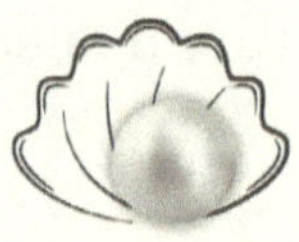

CHAPTER FIVE

IT WAS UNUSUAL FOR DANYELLE'S FATHER to be home during the week, but their water heater needed a plumber's attention, and he wanted to be home in the event there were questions. Danyelle could feel her palms begin to sweat as she approached the den her father used as an office. Danyelle knew her father loved her, but his expectations were so high that she often felt he was unhappy with her. She especially hated disturbing him when he was working, because he became edgy when trying to concentrate. She also knew she had stretched his patience with her constant lobbying to stay where they were. Danyelle gave herself a pep talk as she reached for the doorknob, but her confidence waned as she opened the door and saw her father's furrowed brow.

"Dad, I need to talk to you about something," Danyelle said timidly, as she looked over the computer monitor that partially obscured her father's face.

"Something?" her dad returned with the inflection of a question.

"Yeah, about that job your company wants you to take." Danyelle could tell her dad's focus was elsewhere.

"I already know you don't want to move. You've made that clear," her father responded, anticipating another complaint.

"Well, I don't want to move, but this is about what's going to happen to us if we do—I mean if you take this job," Danyelle said quietly, with a tone of respect, still unsure how she was going to tell him what she knew.

"You don't know the future, Danyelle," her father said, frustrated with his teenage daughter.

"No, dad—you're wrong. I *do* know. I know for sure," Danyelle said, raising her voice, trying to muster strength.

He stopped what he was doing and rolled his office chair out from behind his desk. The sound from the casters reverberated as they rolled across the hardwood floor. At first, he looked down, elbows on his knees, hands folded. He sighed, "Look, Danyelle, I know this is a big deal, picking up and going to somewhere new, but it can be a great adventure. You'll meet new friends, and it can take me to a new level in the company. It opens the door to so many things for us."

"Dad, I'm not saying this for the reason you think. I can't really explain how I know this, but some guy named John Henderson is trying to screw you. The place we'd be moving to, they're going to close it down—I mean the plant. The company is going to close the plant."

Her father looked at her with an expression she rarely saw on her father's face, a look of confusion. "How do you know *John Henderson*? How would you know about the plant?"

"Someone told me, dad, and I can't say who. Please just check it out before you decide. This is really serious," Danyelle pleaded.

"*Someone*?" he pressed.

"Dad, I can't tell you! Just check it out. Please!" Danyelle's emotions bubbled to the surface.

He could see the earnestness in her eyes and decided not to question further. "I promise I will look into it."

Danyelle's father followed through on his promise, and it wasn't long before it all unraveled for John Henderson when it was discovered he'd falsified documents as part of his scheme—he was let go. Danyelle's father was promoted, and Danyelle and her family stayed put.

CHAPTER SIX

THE GIRLS NOW BELIEVED that the pearl's ability to reveal answers was genuine. And, although the overall outcome for Danyelle and her family was positive, their instincts told them it was best to keep what had happened a secret, for fear that if word got out, things could spiral out of control.

Jenny, Danyelle, and Ashley had moved on and scarcely discussed the pearl, until, on a cold October Thursday, life turned another page. Ashley's cousin Mary, newly married at twenty-five years old, was pregnant and thrilled at the prospect of starting a family that had long been a dream. She had posted the exciting news and began the time-honored process of transforming a small third bedroom into a nursery. The families were so happy for Mary and rallied around her and her husband. As cliché as it sounds, Mary glowed, but an event lay ahead that would test the couple's mettle.

Mary was returning from Home Depot after another preparedness-shopping spree; she was struggling to fit her key into the lock with arms weighed down by heavy bags. Just before she gained entry, her phone began ringing—a ring-tone she'd set up specifically to alert her when the OB-GYN was calling. The door swung open wildly, rebounding against the doorstop as she stumbled into the entryway. She managed to answer the phone as she dropped the bags to the hardwood floor. As she listened to the nurse, her rosy complexion faded, becoming colorless. The doctor wanted to see her as soon as it could be arranged. The appointment was set for the following day.

The doctor was kind and patient but explained the results of a blood test in stark, unambiguous language. "The child has a seventy-five percent chance of being born with a serious disability."

Mary could feel herself drifting away. Her rational self knew she should be paying attention to what the doctor was saying, but there was another, deeper, flight-or-fight self that pulled her focus elsewhere. To Mary, the doctor's voice was like a TV that had been left on in an upstairs bedroom—a faint, distant noise.

"Mary, did you hear what I said? You shouldn't lose hope. Mary!" the doctor raised her voice, trying to bring Mary back to the moment at hand.

The world now looked different; it had turned gray and murky, like a fog that had come to stay. She knew that she would have the baby regardless of the test results and that her husband would stand with her, but a sadness had grabbed her by the throat, and she needed to grieve and talk to those who loved her.

—·—

Ashley was in the room when her mother, Mary's aunt Linda, took Mary's call. Before the discussion was over, Ashley saw her mother turn pale and could hear Mary's faint weeping, even though she was sitting five feet away from her mother.

"Mom and dad are planning to sell the farm and move here to help. They love that farm, and I feel guilty, but they won't hear of anything else," Mary's voice broke again.

"It's no one's fault, Mary. Not yours, not anyone's," Ashley heard her mother say as she tried to comfort Mary.

"If only we knew for sure, even if it is hard news," Mary said, frustrated by the unfairness.

"I'm so sorry; we'll do everything we can to help. We love you. Call me day or night, Mary. Do you hear me? Day or night!" were the last words Ashley heard her mother say before disconnecting the call.

After her mother repeated the full story, Ashley called Jenny and Danyelle.

"I don't know if you would call it a "last resort," but she really needs help. She feels guilty that her parents are going to sell their farm and move here, and she's scared for her baby. She's desperate," Ashley explained as their FaceTime session continued.

"We have to try to help," Jenny answered.

"Guys—we agreed we should keep this a secret," Danyelle murmured.

"I know. I remember—and I feel bad asking—but what would you do? If you guys could have heard Mary . . ." Ashley stopped mid-sentence.

"Don't feel bad, Ash. If it were my family, I would want to do something, too," Jenny reassured Ashley.

"I guess you have to make the decision, Jenny," Danyelle said after a moment's silence.

"Then I say we do it." Jenny's voice brightened. "But how do we go about it? My parents don't know, and Mary will think we're crazy."

"Well, maybe we give Mary a care package and see if she'll talk to us," Danyelle suggested.

"I could make mom's lemon-glazed bunt cake," Jenny followed.

"Ooo—I'm all for the cake," Ashley laughed, trying to break away from the intensity for a moment.

"The cake is for Mary, Ash," Danyelle scolded.

"Maybe she'll share," Ashley said as they all laughed.

CHAPTER SEVEN

ASHLEY'S MOM DROPPED THE GIRLS at Mary's home and waited until Mary let them in. They were toting toiletries, a Starbucks gift card, the lemon cake, and—if they could reason a way to introduce the subject—the oyster's gift.

Mary smiled when she saw what the girls were carrying, but her eyes told a different story. Her expression couldn't mask their redness or hide her skin's irritation—she'd been crying again.

"It was so nice of you to think about me," Mary said, as she closed the door behind her visitors.

"We brought you some stuff," Ashley offered as they walked to the kitchen.

"Aww," Mary uttered, touched by their thoughtfulness.

"We know you're having a tough time," Danyelle said, reaching for Mary's hand.

Danyelle's touch caused Mary to sigh deeply, and she hesitated to respond as her emotions began to get the better of her.

"Let's slice that beautiful cake," she said, after gathering herself. "I'll make a pot of coffee as well."

Mary complimented Jenny on her baking achievement as they sat around the kitchen table, though Mary ate very little. The balance of the conversation consisted of little more than small talk, which finally drew to a close when none of them knew how to bridge a moment of silence that filled the room.

"We have something to ask you . . . I mean, *tell* you," Ashley said, not knowing how else to broach the subject.

"I'm sorry?" Mary said, not certain she heard Ashley correctly.

"I don't know . . . Jenny, Danyelle—how do I say this?"

"Mary, what if you could ask a question—only one—and be sure of the answer? Would that help?" Jenny said, trying to take things further.

"We know this sounds crazy, but if you trust us, we think maybe we can help you," Danyelle followed.

"I still don't understand: How could you possibly know the answer to a question I might ask, especially if it's about the future?" Mary asked, confused at what the girls were trying to communicate.

"This is so hard. What would you ask—I mean, if you believed us?" Ashley added.

"I think you know what I would ask." Mary stopped and then continued, "I would want to know if my baby will be born with a disability."

Ashley nodded and looked at her friends. "So, how do we tell her before she kicks us out and calls our parents?"

"Tell me what?" Mary asked, like a mother would her child.

"I don't know what to say, Mary. This is an 'I don't believe a word you're saying' story. I mean, if it hadn't happened to me, I wouldn't believe it. So, all I know to do is tell you, and, then, like Ash said, you can kick us out and call our moms," Jenny said as she crossed and uncrossed her fingers in nervous habit.

"I still don't understand, but I want to hear what you're talking about," Mary responded after a brief interlude.

Jenny talked about the set of events she had relayed to her friends those weeks ago at their lunch table at school. Though nervous, she was clear and calm, on pitch; she barely looked away from Mary. When she finished, she took a sip of her coffee, which, by this time, was hardly even warm.

Mary looked at each of the girls, perhaps to decide if this was a badly construed practical joke, but she saw no false expression.

"Am I allowed to see it?" Mary asked succinctly.

"The pearl?" Jenny returned.

"Yes . . . please," Mary affirmed.

"Of course." Jenny smiled.

Jenny stood and walked to the backpack she had left in the foyer. She removed the silken handkerchief her grandmother had given her. When she returned to the table, she placed the faded lavender cloth on the table and carefully uncovered what once had lain in the mollusk's shell she buried those months ago.

"I've never seen a gem or stone more beautiful," Mary said as she looked at its gleaming surface. "And you don't think it's evil in nature?"

"No. Don't ask me how I know, but I think it is a little fragment of love," Jenny answered, surprised at her word choice.

"That's pretty," Danyelle whispered.

Mary continued examining the pearl, looked up, and spoke softly. "I want to try."

"To ask a question?" Jenny asked in an equally quiet voice.

"Yes, to ask a question," Mary responded.

"Maybe we should move to the sofa. The last time, I felt kind of dizzy, and I don't want to end up on your floor."

"No shit," Ashley agreed.

"Ashley!" Mary admonished.

"Sorry, I mean I *agree*," Ashley said timidly.

Once settled into the soft upholstered furniture, Jenny took the pearl in hand. Mary needed no help forming her question.

"Will my unborn child be born with a disability?" Mary asked clearly.

The air in the room stirred, as if an outside door had been opened. Then, in a repeat of the first session, Jenny's eyes closed before opening again, and, after a moment, she began speaking in her wise old voice. "When born, your child will be free of any disability, either physical or mental. An employee at the lab that processed your blood broke protocol and made an error. You should request a new test."

"My God," Mary said after she considered what Jenny had said. "My God," she repeated. "Can this possibly be true?"

"Can *what* be true?" Jenny followed, once again unaware of the answer she'd given.

"Everything Jenny said about my dad and his job was 100%," Danyelle offered to Mary, skipping past Jenny's question.

"What did I say?" Jenny pressed.

"You really don't remember?" Mary asked.

"No. The last thing I remember is holding the pearl and then drifting away. It sounded like I was walking on the shore—you know, the waves," Jenny explained.

"In so many words, you said the baby will be okay and that someone at the lab who processed my blood made a mistake," Mary responded with an inflection of hope.

"By the way, do you feel okay?" Mary asked.

"A little tired, but okay."

"Good," Mary said, with a smile. "I really don't know what to think, but I'm going to call my doctor."

Mary promised a second time to keep what had happened to herself as she bade the girls goodbye.

On Monday morning, Mary called her doctor and requested a retest—from another lab. Though the doctor thought the request was a symptom of Mary's refusal to accept the original results, she agreed. In two days' time, there were new results. There was no indication of any problems with the baby. The doctor was apologetic—and baffled.

CHAPTER EIGHT

THE PEARL HAD REMAINED in its musical hiding place for several months more, when another cry for help unexpectedly arose. Mary had a friend in trouble who desperately needed a question answered. Mary hadn't broken her promise to not speak of the pearl, but she did approach Ashley.

"So, Mary has a friend, a good friend, who is totally struggling. Mary didn't tell her about us or about the pearl, but Mary asked if we would think about it. I guess there are a lot of people who need help," Ashley said, waiting to hear what Jenny and Danyelle had to say.

"I'm not saying we should, but what is the question this time?" Danyelle asked.

"That's the thing—it's pretty intense," Ashley answered without answering.

"Yeah, so what is her friend's question?" Danyelle asked again.

"She wants to know if she should take her father off of life support," Ashley mumbled, like she didn't want to answer.

"You can't be serious," Danyelle said in disbelief.

"I know, but . . . ,"

"But *what*?" Danyelle interrupted.

"But, like her dad has been wasting away for a long time, and they're keeping him alive like he's a lab rat or something. He didn't leave one of those wills or whatever they're called."

No one knew what to say until Jenny asked, "Can we talk to her? I mean, before we decide?"

"That's a good idea," Ashley answered. "I'm sure Mary can set something up."

Three days later Mary, Ashley, Danyelle, and Jenny were FaceTiming with a woman named Kari.

"I trust Mary, otherwise, I wouldn't be . . . I wouldn't be asking for help—how can I say—help of *this kind*. I don't believe in the things Mary described, but it's my father, and I don't know what to do." Kari stopped talking a minute to steady herself. "He was in a terrible car accident. Some kid using a cell phone crossed into dad's lane and hit him head-on. The boy died, and I feel for his family, but my daddy has been in a coma for eleven months. They don't think he'll come out of it. I'm his only child, and he's my daddy." Again, she stopped—this time, walking away from the phone for a few minutes. "I'm sorry. This is so hard. I still get angry, and I'm just so sad. My dad intended to fill out the paper-work . . . the living will, so this kind of thing didn't have to fall on me. My mom passed when I was very young, so it's just me and daddy. Anyway, he never got around to it."

"I totally get why you don't believe this. We asked Mary to explain it to you because we thought you might not want to talk after you heard the story, but here you are," Jenny started. "So, we are really scared to try to help you with this. We have helped with some pretty serious stuff, but nothing like this, and we don't feel good about answering your question."

"What you've said already makes me feel better. As I said, I have faith in Mary, but I was worried she had fallen for some scam. I like your sincerity and judgment—it gives me a sense of peace. Would it help if I told you the question I want to ask has changed?"

"Changed how?" Danyelle asked.

"Last night, I decided this wasn't something I could put in anyone's hands. It's *my* decision to make," Kari said, beginning to sob. "I've decided to ask the doctors to turn off the machines. But I want to ask if daddy will be okay when he passes."

"I'm so sorry for you, Kari. I don't know how you're keeping it together," Ashley said, softly.

"I'm really sorry, too, Kari, but I think you're right about deciding for yourself what to do," Danyelle said, relieved that Kari had changed the question she wanted to ask.

"I'm really sorry, too," Jenny added, "and I don't know if I'll give a good answer to your question, but I think we should try. One thing, though: I don't know where we should meet."

"I've been thinking about that while you were talking. How about at my house . . . if everyone is comfortable with that? After all, I'm the one who's been the go-between for Kari," Mary offered.

"Have you managed to get any rest?" Mary asked Kari as she stooped to place a tray, loaded with teapot and pastries, on the large ottoman occupying space at the room's center.

"Not really, and I'm still skeptical and wondering why I'm even here. Don't get me wrong: I appreciate everything you're doing to help," Kari said, "but I'm going to meet with the doctors on Monday, so they can explain the process . . . I mean how they pull daddy off the machines. So you'll have to forgive me if I'm not myself."

"Aww, I wish there was something else that could be done," Jenny responded, somehow feeling guilty, though there was no justification for such a feeling.

"It's okay, Jenny. I've done so much crying over the last few months, I'm surprised I have a tear left. Every time I think I've made sense of things, I slip back again. Just talking about it makes me feel like I'm going to lose it, so, before I do, can you again explain to me how this works?" Kari asked in a hurried tone.

"There isn't much to it, Kari. I take hold of the pearl, and then you ask your question."

"I hate to sound curt, but can we get started before I lose my nerve?" Kari said in return.

"You sound fine, and I'm ready," Jenny said as she uncovered the pearl and took it in hand.

"It is extraordinary," Kari commented, staring at the glowing pearl before clearing her throat and nervously asking, "Will my daddy be all right when he dies?"

Jenny's transition from teen to sage followed the familiar pattern. "Your father has already begun his journey from this world to the next. When he passes, his soul will be free to move wholeheartedly to the unseen side. To your question, he shall be embarking on an adventure of joy, learning, and growth unlike any we can imagine. He shall be lovingly welcomed and surrounded by many who have gone before—even relatives he never knew in this world. He will be supremely happy but will never lose his link to you and the incredible love you share. You will know when his spirit is near."

With her last word yet gracing the room, Jenny came back to them, to find them silent. "Did something go wrong?" Jenny asked, always feeling like the odd one out.

"Nothing's wrong, Jenny . . . I mean nothing went wrong. I'm sorry—I have to go," Kari said as her emotions once again began to get the better of her. "Thank you—all of you."

Before leaving, Kari embraced Mary and each of the girls. Though she knew something remarkable had happened, her lingering doubt still colored her perspective. By Monday afternoon, Kari's father no longer had the benefit of the medical technology that had kept his body alive for those many months. He passed away one hour later with Kari at his side.

"I know this has been hard, Kari, but I want you to know how brave I think you've been," Meredith, the nurse on duty, shared.

"I don't feel so brave," Kari responded.

"You know, I try to separate myself from my patients, at least a little bit, because I find it difficult to handle the emotions, but I haven't been able to with you and your father. On the way to work, I stopped by the park to try—I don't know—I guess to try to make some sense of this. I know you're going to think I'm crazy, but as I sat there, I swear to you, I heard a voice—a man's voice—that sounded so kind. It—I mean, *he*—said to pick a flower. I didn't see anything at first, but then I noticed this tiny wildflower at the base of a willow tree. I don't know if I was supposed to, but I picked it. Somehow, I knew I needed to give it to you," she said as she pulled a tissue from her pocket and unveiled the beautiful early spring bloom.

"Oh, my God," Kari gasped. "A violet. That's the first flower my dad ever gave me. He always said I was even prettier than a flower. He would pick one for me each time they bloomed," Kari said as she took it from the Kleenex. This time, Kari cried tears of joy, and she remembered what Jenny had said—that she would know when her father's spirit was near.

CHAPTER NINE

ANOTHER REQUEST, ANOTHER DECISION. Mary knew of a woman whose question concerned a possible surgery for her daughter and asked if the girls would entertain answering it. Not surprisingly, the girls said, "Yes."

On a Saturday afternoon, Mary again played host and met the latest participant at the door.

"Girls, this is Susan." Mary smiled as she offered Susan a seat.

"Thank you," Susan quietly answered, as if she were a thousand miles away. "Thanks for having me."

"Are you okay?" Danyelle asked, sensing Susan's hesitancy.

"Yes. I'm sorry if I seem distant. It's just that life has been so difficult lately. It's hard to know what to do," Susan answered in the same, detached voice.

"Are you sure you're ready for this?" Mary asked, sensing what Danyelle had detected.

"Yes," Susan answered in an elevated, almost aggravated, tone. "On top of everything else, I'm having relationship issues. My husband and I aren't getting along, and I feel lost."

"Maybe we should do this another time," Mary suggested, now growing more hesitant.

"No, please. I really need this," Susan insisted.

"It's okay; we want to help," Danyelle offered, torn by her own conflicted feelings.

"I'm sorry I'm so emotional, but I really need to know," Susan answered, more calmly this time. "Can we get started?"

"Sure . . . no problem," Jenny answered quickly, thinking it would help Susan if she moved things along. Jenny unveiled the gleaming gold globe and took it in hand. "You can ask your question anytime you're ready."

Susan looked intently at Jenny and posed her question: "Should I take my own life?"

Danyelle and Ashley gasped in unison, but this didn't stop Jenny from answering the question.

"*No*," Jenny said, sternly, in a pitch that was unfamiliar, even for elder Jenny.

The room grew completely quiet, and no one knew if Jenny would utter another word, when she suddenly broke the silence, continuing in a sincere yet caring timbre.

"Life is a gift like no other. But some would scarcely call it a gift but see it instead as an endless exercise in drudgery. It is a gift that requires perspective, an ability to understand that the beauty of the senses—the range of emotions, the varied feelings that are part of the material world—are unparalleled. To hold a child in your arms and then to wish that child farewell when grown, to feel the warm breezes of summer and the bitter winds of winter, to share a feast with family or the pain of scarcity and hunger, to feel the wonder of love gained and the devastation of love lost—the dichotomy of life is a wonder. All who arrive amidst this seeming chaos have a destiny. Ending life before achieving what was meant to be creates waves of sadness in this world and in the one we don't see. Emotional pain of the nature you are experiencing is debilitating, but it is important to remember that the sun will rise again. Should you choose to stay the course, you will emerge from your divorce, meet another, and have a fulfilling, lifelong relationship. Further, though you don't yet realize it, you are pregnant with your second child, and taking your life will rob you and the world of a child who will grow to touch many through her extraordinary musical talents. All who tread path on this Earth can, at one time or another, become overwhelmed with life's difficulties. You are not alone—carefully consider your decision."

When Jenny opened her eyes, she found that Susan was sobbing deeply. Jenny looked to her friends, each of whom was visibly upset.

"I'm so sorry that I wasn't honest. This isn't like me . . . really, it isn't. But I didn't think you would accept me if you knew my true question," she said as she stood and gathered her things.

"Susan, are you going to be okay?" Danyelle asked as she stood and sharpened her gaze to meet Susan's.

"You don't have to worry about me. I'm ashamed of what I was considering."

"Don't feel that way, Susan. There is nothing to be ashamed of," Danyelle said before Susan walked to the front door with Mary at her side.

Ashley and Danyelle explained to Jenny what had happened. Although Susan had walked away with a newfound view of life, they knew now there was a new element to consider when answering questions—people sometimes lie.

CHAPTER TEN

ROBERT IMAN SAT AT HIS DESK staring at the paperwork in front of him, but not reading. A professor, he had long studied ancient history—the customs, the cultures, the world's religions, the rise of empires and their demise, but he was especially attracted to lore, mythology, and mysticism. He had traveled the world in study of his passions, searching for a breakthrough that would pluck him from obscurity and place him alongside his famous colleagues, and he hoped to garner all the trappings of such notoriety. There was an urgency to his work, for the years had passed like a snowfall that holds a sparkling beauty in its youth but quickly wanes with the rise of the next day's sun. He was desperately searching for one true thing that would set him apart.

For thousands of years, seawater pearls had been found in the Indian Ocean. Though the specimens harvested were not, on balance, as impressive as those found in other quarters of the world, there were exceptions. The most notable being a gold pearl found sometime in the early third century. There were references to the majesty of this precious object in the few volumes that survived that time and place. They described its beauty and spherical perfection at length, but, in latter writings, there was mention of curious incidents in which the possessor of the pearl, a provincial sultan, would enter a speaking dream-like state when holding the orb and addressing a request or indeterminant phrase—a question. Rumors that this local dignitary had a unique power grew until a formidable neighboring ruler pressed an invasion to conquer land, resources, and, of course, the coveted gold object. Before it could be taken by the invading horde, the sultan threw it back into the sea from which it came and was beheaded for his impudence.

Note of the pearl's reappearance did not occur for another 200 years, when a wealthy merchant acquired it while shucking fresh oysters. He was so enthralled with it, he seldom let it out of his presence. It was rumored he slept with it. He, too, gained a reputation for being able to answer questions after entering what was referred to as "... a stupor." The pearl later vanished under questionable circumstances.

Over the course of time, the pearl appeared and disappeared, leaving scant traces in various documents and publications. Professor Iman had studied every account, every sighting, every instance he could digest and felt it was time for the pearl to reveal itself. He was convinced the pearl was no myth and that it held a power—a power that could be exploited, and he intended to find it.

CHAPTER ELEVEN

WITH LITTLE IN THE WAY OF PAUSE, the girls decided to entertain another request—out of all people, it came from Susan. Naturally, Mary, who had taken on the role of quasi-guardian, was incredulous.

"I know I have zero credibility, and I've no right to even ask. I would have never called, but this is about two men I know, two incredible human beings who are on the brink of making a life-changing decision. And I'm telling you, the world could wind up worse off than it already is," Susan rattled off, without taking a breath.

Mary let out a sigh. "Who are these men?"

Susan took a deep breath, relieved that Mary was willing to hear more and that she hadn't disconnected the call. "They are brothers, twins, James and Johnathan Colman—and they're also priests. They have traveled the globe for years, going to places no one else will, places in turmoil. They save lives and ignore the danger to themselves, but they're having a crisis of faith. I've tried to encourage them, but I don't know how to respond to their basic questions. I don't know if anyone besides Jenny can."

"What do you mean, 'basic questions'?"

"Spiritual questions, good-and-evil kind of questions," Susan answered.

"And this isn't a trick?" Mary asked directly.

"I can't blame you for asking, but I swear to you, this is no trick."

"Mary, are you still there?" Susan asked when Mary didn't say anything further.

"Yes, I'm still here. Look, I can't promise anything, but I'll let the girls know you called."

"Thank you—that's all I'm asking."

"I'll let you know. Yes, goodbye," Mary hung up the phone. It was obviously difficult to return to trusting Susan, but her sincerity was compelling, as was the thought of hearing the answers to the proposed questions.

————

"You can't deny she has some balls," Ashley said after Mary broke the news.

"Must you, Ashley?" All Mary could do was shake her head.

"You know what I mean," Ashley smiled.

"Yes, Ashley," Mary said, letting it go.

"Yeah, but can we trust her?" Danyelle interrupted.

"If it helps, I did google the names she gave me, and they—I mean the brothers—are real. Everything I read agrees with what she said. They seem like amazing people," Mary shared as she folded laundry still warm from the dryer.

"So, I know I'm always the one saying, 'Let's do it,' but let's do it. If they're helping people, like Susan said, we have to," Jenny replied." The oyster said to follow my heart."

"You're too nice," Ashley laughed. "But that's why we love you—I'm with Jenny."

"You're doing all the hard work, Jenny. If you're good, so am I," Danyelle joined.

"Okay. I'll call Susan and let her know. One more thing, ladies: We need to tell your parents what's going on. I can't keep hosting these . . . these secret sessions," Mary insisted.

"Can we wait until after the brothers?" Jenny asked.

"I'll go that far, but no further," Mary said firmly.

The girls grumbled. "You have to help us talk to them," Danyelle said, worried what her father would say.

"I promise—I'll be right beside you," Mary said, in a supporting voice.

<hr>

"Hi," Mary said as she welcomed the brothers. "This is Ashley, Danyelle, and Jenny."

"It's nice to meet you. I'm James, and this is Johnathan," James said as he extended his hand to Mary and each of the girls. Johnathan followed in kind.

After everyone took their seats, Johnathan spoke. "As I'm sure Susan mentioned, my brother and I are at a crossroads. We are struggling with our faith—with our beliefs. Both of us feel, I'd guess you'd say, a level of foolishness believing the questions we have could be answered in this way. I don't wish to convey offense—to any of you—but were we not at this point in our lives, I doubt we would be here. I don't know—maybe our apprehension is partly rooted in our shame."

"You have to understand, it has been extraordinarily hard for years now," James added.

"I don't want to make you feel like you're sitting on the witness stand," Mary led, "but we have been deceived in the past, and Susan didn't provide much detail. So, can you tell us more about your story—what brought you to this point?"

James turned to Johnathan as if to silently ask who the spokesman should be. Without James uttering a word aloud, Johnathan seemed to understand he was elected.

"Where to start?" Johnathan opened. "We began traveling the world together after graduating from the seminary. Over the years, we've been to China, Africa, Europe, the Middle East, South America, and several points in America. We follow disasters of all kinds, natural *and* those created by our fellow men. As devastating as a hurricane or earthquake can be, what has broken our hearts and spirits is what we've seen brother do to brother. Torture, hatred, cruelty beyond imagining. In the beginning, we thought we could change this through love and caring and kind example, but, as time has gone by, it has become apparent nothing will stop this tide of human brutality when power, wealth, and revenge are part of the equation. No country, no region, no race, no creed is immune. We've been jailed, beaten, and forced to leave communities that desperately needed assistance. After seeing this repeat many times, we've lost our belief, our faith. I don't know—perhaps we're simply worn down."

Johnathan's last word floated in the air and resurrected faint memories of lessons taught in history class of ethnic cleansing, war, and vicious dictators. When the girls read about those places and events, they seemed so distant, so unreal. It was hard to believe there were people on the ground trying to make a difference against a wave of inhumanity.

Danyelle was first to speak. "It's hard for me to imagine what you've seen, but I don't think you should feel ashamed to be human."

Johnathan bowed his head, and James patted him on the back. "Thank you, Danyelle, and you're right in what you say, but we never thought we would question our very foundation." After a pause, James continued. "Are you still willing to entertain our questions?"

"Absolutely," Jenny answered. "It's the first time we're meeting with two people at the same time. If it's okay with you, please give me a short break between questions."

The brothers nodded in agreement. "Johnathan, I think you should go first."

"Give me just a second," Jenny said, as she removed the pearl and tightened her grip. "I'm ready."

Johnathan exhaled deeply. "Does the devil exist?"

Jenny began speaking. "There is a dark force that thrives on our selfishness, our greed, our hate, our pettiness, our prejudice, our fear, and our insecurities. Without these contributions, the darkness cannot exist; it shrinks away. The darkness is cowardly and speaks in lies, but if we give it a foothold, it can grow and flourish. This force wields no true power, though even well-meaning souls can fall prey when they put their trust in charlatans who understand how to use this force to exploit our base need to believe in falsehoods. Though life's disappointments and difficulties can tempt us to submit to this enemy of love and truth, it is important for each of us to find the better angels within ourselves to take away the fuel the darkness needs to burgeon. In comparison to the vastness of the opposing light, the darkness is but one grain of sand. Nonetheless, even a single grain can cause significant irritation."

When she finished, Jenny felt a stillness and could see in Johnathan's face that he had been profoundly affected. "Are you okay?"

"Yes, Jenny, and thank you."

"Are you sure you can endure another question?" James asked, noticing that Jenny seemed tired and somehow affected by what had been said.

"I'm fine—really, I am. You can ask your question when you're ready," Jenny quietly said, smiling.

"If you're sure," James said before putting forth his question: "Does God really exist?"

In a more insightful, focused voice than Jenny had yet spoken, she began. "Yes, and it is an entity whose description in words is impossible other than to say it is love, though our concept of love pales in comparison to the immenseness of the love that makes up its being. This entity we call 'God,' this loving force, this incredible living energy, is in all of us, in all things, and it is impossible to separate ourselves from it, as we are an extension of it. It is the ultimate gift and is what makes life possible." Breaking from the usual routine, Jenny paused and then continued. "Although it isn't readily apparent, doing good, particularly in the face of evil, generates a resonance that greatly diminishes the dark force—you and your brother have done more to change the hearts of your fellow women and men than you can fathom. Humankind is in its infancy, and children can be very cruel, but, given time, they grow and learn."

When Jenny emerged, all faces were on her. Even her two lifelong friends, who had been with her for each session, looked at her in amazement.

"I am simply astounded," James said, as Johnathan rubbed his eyes. "When we came here, I thought we would learn that these children were misled, or overindulged, but I no longer believe this. There is something special here, something spiritual, something beautiful. Thank you for sharing this with us."

The brothers left that evening as changed men, feeling a purpose once again rising in their hearts. The oyster had said that the pearl was a gift that could change lives, and this night, more than ever, it had.

CHAPTER TWELVE

AS THE EVENING APPROACHED, Mary felt her heart rate quicken, and she found it difficult to focus on what she was doing. She was nervous but was certain they couldn't continue to conduct their sessions in secrecy—it was time to tell the girls' parents. They considered meeting with the parents couple by couple, but, in the end, they elected to meet as a larger group. So tonight, they were all invited to dinner at Mary's house.

"Hi, everyone. Glad you were all able to make it," Mary started. "You remember my husband, Tim?"

"Sure . . . hey, Tim . . . Hi, Tim . . . ," voices rang out around the room.

"So, we have some things to talk about, but, before that, as you can probably tell from these wonderful aromas, I want to let you know we all worked our butts off fixing a nice dinner." Mary and Tim smiled as they put their arms around the anxious but proud trio.

The group gathered around the dining table and shared wilted spinach salad, maple-glazed tenderloin, Potatoes Anna, and blueberry cobbler. By the time dinner was finished, all were drowsy and full, all except the girls, who had eaten judiciously, concerned with how the after-dinner conversation would unfold.

When the families were comfortably sitting in the living room, Mary began speaking, telling from start to finish what she knew and she related what had happened in the other sessions she'd observed. When she was finished, the room was silent. The parents looked as though the stories Mary told had been spoken in a foreign tongue. Danyelle's father was the first to speak. "Danyelle, is this how you knew about my job offer and John Henderson?"

"Yeah. I'm sorry I didn't say something before, but I didn't know how to tell you. I mean, I've been part of this, and, listening to Mary, it still sounds so crazy," Danyelle answered, fighting her dry throat.

"What are you saying? Do you really believe this? This story about a magical pearl?" Jenny's father, Seth, asked in a skeptical tone.

"Believe? Everything tells me 'No,' but Danyelle knew things that were impossible for her to know—I mean *impossible*. And there is one thing I absolutely believe: Danyelle wouldn't lie to me," Danyelle's father responded. Danyelle's heart skipped a beat; she had no idea he thought this about her, let alone would say it aloud in a setting such as this. It brought a smile to her face. To hear her father say, in front of all the others, that he trusted her word, made her want to run to him.

"Look, I'm not accusing anyone of lying, but *a pearl that answers questions*? There must be another explanation. And say I'm wrong, and this thing does have a power. How do we know it's safe? How do we know where this thing came from?" Seth responded sternly.

"Dad, I know you're worried, and I understand why you are, but I'm the one who experiences this, and I know it's a good thing. It helps people. Look what it did for Mary. Dad, don't make this a bad thing, please," Jenny pleaded. Jenny knew her father was doing what he always did. He worried about everything, and it affected her whole family, and, what was worse, Jenny felt afraid all the time, and she detested it. She loved her dad, but she didn't want to navigate life the way he did.

"I hear you, Jenny, but until we have a better understanding of what is going on, you cannot meet with your friends for the purpose of . . . of answering questions using this pearl." Seth made it clear what he expected.

"No, dad—you can't do this! You just can't!" Jenny beseeched, fighting back tears.

"We'll talk about this later," her father demanded with a look she knew all too well.

After hearing their exchange, and letting the room quiet, Ashley's mother, Linda, a soft-spoken woman who had a flair for considering all points of view, spoke. "Seth, I understand your apprehension, and I'm tempted to follow your lead, but perhaps you would be willing to entertain a suggestion. What if we refrain from judgment until we see for ourselves what it's like when Mary and the girls conduct one of their meetings? Lord knows Ashley can be impulsive, but she has good instincts. I know she would have come to me if she felt this pearl was in some way evil. Mary, girls, do you think it would be all right for us to sit in next time—that is, if Jenny's father allows it?"

"I don't see a problem with that," Mary answered, breaking her silence.

"I think that's a great idea, mom," Ashley answered, feeling so proud of her mom, secretly wishing she had inherited her mom's ability to gently persuade. Ashley knew she was much more like her father—a bull in a china shop.

"I totally agree," Danyelle answered as she looked at her parents.

"Seth, would you be willing to try?"

Seth looked at his daughter and saw a longing in her eyes. "I'm willing to try this if Jenny's okay with it and she promises not to have any more sessions until we have had a chance to observe one."

"I think it's a great idea, and cross my heart," Jenny said as she wiped a tear from her cheek and smiled at her father.

"Well, the timing couldn't be more apropos. I was waiting to tell you that I have another friend who is struggling . . . I know—it's like all my friends need help," Mary said with a faint smile.

"What is it this time? I mean we've had a medical crisis—really two. We've had a spiritual crisis. We've had a suicidal woman," Ashley asked, looking at Mary.

"If you want to take it on, this is a matrimonial question."

"We have to," Jenny answered, putting her arm around Ashley, beckoning Danyelle to join them.

"You guys aren't doing it without me," Danyelle declared as she joined her friends' embrace.

CHAPTER THIRTEEN

MARY AGAIN EXPLAINED TO THE GROUP how the first few sessions had unfolded, and she also explained how Jenny communicated the answers—her tone and disposition. Mary hoped her "briefing" would put everyone at ease, though she also knew most parents were professional worriers when their daughters and sons were part of the equation.

"Wow—you said a group would be attending, but, I have to say, this is intimidating," Mary's friend Emma announced as she took in the room.

"I'm sorry. I guess I could have done a better job of explaining things," Mary admitted as she asked everyone to introduce themselves. "The girls' parents are just learning about this and wanted to observe. If it's too much, we can call it off."

Emma again looked around the room and quietly laughed. "I feel like I'm airing my dirty laundry to all the world. No—I still want to move forward."

"I know everyone in this room, and I feel confident what is said here will stay here," Mary responded.

"Mary, we've known each other for some time, and I know you wouldn't have encouraged me to try this if you had any doubts."

Mary smiled. "Emma, can you give us a little background before we get started?"

"Sure," Emma began. "I'm in love with a guy I've been dating for a little more than a year. He proposed two weeks ago, but I told him I had to think about it. I know it hurt him, and it's been tearing me up. The thing is, there's something I can't put my finger on. He's told me next to nothing about his past. When I've asked, he's had a way of sidestepping my questions. But it could also be me—I have a past. I was married once before and went through a rough divorce. It pisses me off because I used to feel confident I could make good judgments about relationships, but my ex did things I never thought possible. So, as hard as it is for me to admit it, I no longer trust my instincts."

Mary moved to embrace her friend before turning to the group. "Do any of you have further questions or comments? Okay, Jenny—I guess you're on," Mary finished after no one spoke up.

"I just need to get the pearl," Jenny spoke calmly, but her demeanor was a façade. Underneath she was as nervous as she had ever been—at least in recent memory. She felt she was standing on a stage under glaring lights and wished she could be anywhere else. Jenny uncovered the pearl and took it in hand. "I'm ready, Emma."

"Should I marry Andrew?" Emma asked as she tapped on her knee nervously.

Each of the parents keenly watched as Jenny morphed into her learned alter ego.

"Your instincts about Andrew are well founded, but not for the reasons you think. Andrew is not his real name, and he can't discuss his past—he is prohibited from doing so. I will not reveal specific detail, but he stood up to testify against a man who belongs to a dangerous criminal organization when no one else would. His words were pivotal in the conviction of this man. Andrew is an amazing, selfless man who puts others first. He's wanted to propose for some time but was extremely apprehensive for obvious reasons. His sponsor convinced him that it was appropriate to marry if he always follows protocol. He intends to tell you, but he can't unless you agree to marry—it's a catch-22. As you might imagine, his brave choice carries with it risk and a life that isn't easy, not only for him but also for you, if you choose to start this journey with him. He loves you deeply but would never fault you for walking away. Given this, you and I both know the answer to your question must come from your heart."

Now a familiar scene, Jenny returned to a room whose air was one of astonishment.

Emma pulled a Kleenex from a box that was sitting on a table next to her chair. "I don't know what to say . . . I'm speechless, and, as my friends would tell you, that takes some doing," Emma said as she mustered a small smile. "I didn't want to say this before we started, but as much as I love and trust Mary, I thought she was full of it," Emma laughed. "I can't say I understand this, but whatever it is, it's amazing. Thank you, from the bottom of my heart. Of all the things I thought might be in Andrew's background, I would have never guessed this."

The parents watched as Emma hugged each of the girls before driving away. With Emma gone, the girls joined the group of adults. Seth was the first to speak. "Sweetheart, I don't pretend to understand this either, but . . . it's incredible. We've talked, and I think I speak for all of us when I say we are willing to let you three continue, taking small steps, but you must include all of us for each session."

"Yes!" Ashley said with a fist pump, feeling a sense of vindication, knowing in her heart that her parents were skeptical.

"It's such a big group. Can just a few of you join us?" Danyelle didn't care for the big production.

"I guess that's up to your parents, Danyelle, but I'm not willing to proceed unless my wife and I are there," Seth rejoined, with Ashley's parents agreeing.

"You're not doing this without us, Danyelle," her parents quickly interjected.

"Okay, okay," Danyelle consented.

"What say you, Jenny?" Seth asked, sounding like a character in an olden novel.

"I'm fine with the plan. I'm just happy that you see what we've said is true. I mean, I know you don't understand it, and I guess I don't either, but I'm happy," Jenny answered, walking over to hug her father.

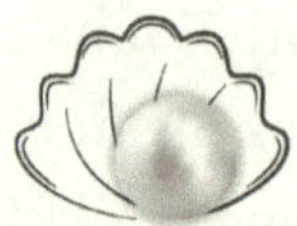

CHAPTER FOURTEEN

"I'LL BE FINE. I'M A LITTLE TIRED, but I'm happy and feel like riding. It's not far," Jenny said as she labored to remove her bicycle from the carrier mounted on the back of her father's car. Jenny rode everywhere she could. Cycling kept her in shape and helped her clear her mind.

"Come straight home."

"I will. Don't worry." Jenny smiled broadly as she shoved off, waving to her mom and dad.

"Proud of you, Jenny," her dad said, waving back.

Ashley, Danyelle, their families, and Mary watched Jenny ride away.

The breeze was freshening, and the air carried with it the promise of Spring. Jenny had the odd sense that a new chapter in her life was beginning. Jenny knew her parents would want to talk further, but their initial reactions made her feel hopeful, and Jenny felt she was using the pearl to make a difference. She often struggled to feel happy, but on this day, she truly did—like at this moment, all in the world was right. As she pedaled onward, she noticed, just ahead, a van had pulled off the road. When she got closer, she could see that a man was in the process of placing a jack under the vehicle. Usually, a flat tire accompanied this exercise, but the tires looked fine.

She had slowed almost to a stop as she approached, when something in her gut sent out a warning. Jenny stood so that she could push down hard. For a moment, she took her eyes off the broken-down van to focus on gaining speed, and, when she turned to judge her distance, a man grabbed her firmly and lifted her off the bicycle's seat. The bike rolled a few feet further, wobbled, and fell to the ground. Jenny fought hard but was unable to free herself. Suddenly she felt a distinct jab. In a matter of seconds, her vision blurred, her limbs dropped, and a terrible blackness overcame her.

She momentarily came to while being wrestled from the van, but her brief intersection with consciousness was short-lived before darkness again prevailed.

When she opened her eyes again, she found herself on her side, lying on a thin mattress, looking across a dusty floor. The drug-induced hangover and odd perspective made her feel like a seasick passenger who had been stuffed below deck. Jenny closed her eyes again, falling into an unnatural sleep. She dreamt that her pearl was rolling down an incline toward a fissure that her dream sense told her was bottomless. But in typical nightmare fashion, she found her legs heavy and unresponsive; she watched helplessly as the pearl rolled to the slab's edge and disappeared.

CHAPTER FIFTEEN

"DID JENNY COME BACK to your house after we left?" Seth asked Mary.

"No . . . what's wrong . . . isn't she home?"

"She isn't home—not yet, anyway," Seth answered with a worried, almost fearful, voice.

"What time is it? Maybe she's still on her way," Mary said as she looked at her watch.

"No, she should have been here by now, unless she stopped on her way. I'm going to call Danyelle and Ashley; she's probably with them," Seth reasoned. "Did she take the pearl with her? I wasn't paying attention."

"She's always careful to take it with her. Seth, you call Danyelle, and I'll call Ashley," Mary insisted.

"Thank you . . . I know I drive everyone crazy with my worry, but . . ." Seth's voice trailed off.

"I'm sure it's okay. I'll call you back in two minutes," Mary said, hurrying the end of the conversation.

"Ashley hasn't heard from her," Mary blurted as soon as Seth answered the call.

"Danyelle hasn't spoken to her since we were at your place," Seth told Mary. "Something is wrong, Mary."

"You call the police, and I'm going to drive the route she would have taken. I'll see you shortly," Mary said without hesitating.

———

Mary pulled into Jenny's driveway and found Seth and Beth waiting. "What did the police say?"

"Where is she, Mary?" Beth asked frantically, not realizing Mary had asked a question.

"I don't know. We need to try to make sense of this. Where would she have gone?" Mary asked as she held Beth in her arms.

"The police said we needed to give it a little time. That teenagers often take detours and show up within a few hours," Seth said, shaking his head.

"Jenny isn't *that* teenager. Hey, doesn't Linda know someone on the force . . . someone she went to school with?" Mary said, pulling back to look at Beth.

"Linda?" Beth asked, not putting two and two together.

"Ashley's mom, my Aunt Linda."

"I can't think right now . . . I do remember her talking about someone . . . is it Ben?" Beth said, wiping tears from her face.

"Let's call her, like *now*. Maybe she can get him involved," Mary said, taking Beth by the arm.

———

With Ben's influence, the police began an unofficial investigation. In the days following Jenny's disappearance, her bicycle was found in a patch of high grass well off the road. The stretch where the detectives discovered the bike was desolate—no doorbell or surveillance cameras to lend an eye. Though there was little in the way of evidence, the case was now classified as an abduction. Preparations were made to trace a kidnapper's call, but, weeks later, no such call had arrived. The FBI was contacted, and Agent Janice Davis was dispatched. She gathered every essential detail, with one exception—no one knew how to bring up the subject of the pearl, for fear that mentioning it would cast doubt and cloud the investigation.

CHAPTER SIXTEEN

"I DON'T UNDERSTAND HOW YOU KNEW I had the pearl," Jenny quietly uttered, not expecting an answer.

"Maybe you've heard the phrase 'It's a small world,' or maybe you've heard this one: 'Loose lips sink ships,' he asked as he looked about the room.

"What does that have to do with anything?" Jenny asked, playing along for the moment.

"As it happens, I came to know one of the women you helped. She audited one of my classes and later invited me to a going-away party—she recently secured a grant to travel to a very remote village to further her studies. The party ran well into the night, as did the drinking, and a small group stayed to discuss ancient myths. I casually mentioned my pet project about a mysterious gold pearl, and her eyes lit up. I doubt if she remembered what she said the morning after, but when her inhibitions were down, she spoke of her meeting with you and your friends. She unwittingly told me all I needed to know to allow me to formulate a plan. For what it's worth, I wouldn't judge her too harshly. As she conveyed the story's detail, it was clear she wasn't over the loss of her father."

Jenny lowered her head and shook it gently—Kari. She felt a sense of betrayal but knew in her heart it was inevitable that word would eventually spread.

"I just want to go home," Jenny pleaded. "I just want to go home."

"I know you do, but as I've been saying, before that can happen, you need to help me," Professor Iman answered, trying to project a sense of concern in his voice.

"I've told you I can't give you the pearl," Jenny said in frustration.

"I don't think that's true, but before we address that subject, there is another task I need your help with."

"What task?" Jenny asked.

"I need you to provide answers to questions. This will do three things. First, it will prove to me that the pearl and you are able to accurately provide answers. Secondly, it will enhance my credibility. Lastly, it will help generate a much-needed influx of funds."

"But I told you I can only answer one question for you," Jenny grumbled.

"I don't like your attitude, and the more you fight me, the longer you'll be here, away from your family," he responded firmly.

"I'm sorry . . . I'm really tired," Jenny replied, softening her voice.

"That's more like it. Jennifer, these aren't *my* questions. These questions will be posed by my clients."

"Are you saying people are coming *here* to ask their questions?" Jenny hoped for a chance to communicate her plight.

"No, no. Through the miracle of the internet and a very special VPN connection, questions will be asked and answered," he said, suspecting why Jenny had asked.

"Can't you just ask your most important question? I promise, I'll answer it, go home, and won't say a thing to anyone," Jenny begged.

"Not to worry, my dear. Before you and I have finished our work, I will ask that question, but we have time. We start tomorrow," he said, turning to leave the room.

"Rise and shine, Jenny." The sound of his voice remotely registered in Jenny's fatigued mind. As she wakened further, she remembered her plight, and a wave of nausea swept over her; her skin became clammy and cold. She didn't react to his command but lay still, cocooned in the sleeping bag he'd provided.

"Get up, Jenny," he repeated in a firmer voice. Jenny remained still, clenching her fists.

"I said, 'Get up!'" he barked loudly while shaking her. Jenny took a swing at his arm. "Look, we can do this the hard way, but keep in mind, the longer you resist, the longer your time with me."

Jenny slowly lifted herself off the uncovered mattress lying on the bare tile floor. "Can I please have a shower?"

"I'll grant your request after we've helped our first participant," he answered unconvincingly.

"Really?" Jenny asked sarcastically.

"Really," he repeated, ignoring her attitude. In 30 minutes, we have our first appointment. There's a tray with cereal and juice on your table. You have just enough time to eat and fix yourself up."

Jenny ate reluctantly, consuming only half of the meager offering. She pulled her hair into a bun and futilely attempted to wash the dark circles from beneath her eyes. As she patted her face dry, she stared at herself in the mirror and silently wished she'd never accepted the pearl, despite the good she and her friends had done through it.

———

Jenny was positioned off camera while the professor spoke to someone he referred to as a colleague. "I see you've made the required deposit."

"And if I'm not satisfied?" the man, who bore a heavy accent, asked in response to the professor's statement.

"As I communicated earlier, your satisfaction is guaranteed. The funds will not be transferred until you bless the transaction."

"All right. I wanted to hear you say it again; $50,000 is a great deal of money to pay to have a question answered."

"It is, but I understand you will make many many times that," the professor retorted.

The client didn't respond to the professor's last statement but instead moved the conversation ahead. "So how do we go about this?"

"Give me a moment on this side," the professor responded, turning toward Jenny, who had already taken the pearl in hand. "We're prepared to answer your question anytime you're ready."

The client cleared his voice. "Will I win my patent case with the Indian government?"

The professor watched with fascination as Jenny entered her trance-like state. "You will win your patent battle, but there will be a condition. The governmental body making the ruling will give partial rights to a competitor who filed a similar patent. This will require you to share thirteen percent of the profits you gain."

The man's facial expression changed. "This is momentous news. I was concerned they would rule in the opposite. This clarifies the approach I need to take moving forward. The announcement is due in one week. If all is as you say, I will relinquish the funds," the man said in an elevated, excited voice.

"Excellent," the professor followed. "Yes, yes. It's been a pleasure . . . goodbye."

Jenny was just recovering when the professor took the pearl, escorted her back to her room, and thanked her for what he called her *performance*.

"Can I go home now?" Jenny asked as he prepared to shut the door.

"If you continue to handle yourself as you did today, your stay with me will be quite short."

CHAPTER SEVENTEEN

DESPITE THEIR EFFORTS, the police had made little progress. They had no way of knowing that Jenny had been transported to a different town. And Kari, the woman who'd put Jenny at risk, was on international assignment and had no idea what had transpired.

More than two months had elapsed and all who loved Jenny were suffering deeply, imagining the worst, not knowing what to do. Ashley and Danyelle were no exception; they were beside themselves not knowing how to help their lifelong friend. Their performance in school fell off dramatically, as did their attendance. Both were seeing therapists and grappling with their emotions, feeling an unfounded guilt for what had happened—both feeling Jenny would somehow save them if the positions were reversed.

"Mom called that police guy she knows, but there is nothing new," Ashley told Danyelle.

"There has got to be something we can do. Jenny would have the National Guard on it if it were you or me," Danyelle responded in frustration.

"I think we should go back to where the police found her bike. There has to be something more," Ashley all but demanded.

"But the police do this every day, and, where they found Jenny's bike, I mean, like, there is *nothing* on that stretch," Danyelle said with hopelessness.

"It doesn't matter. Today, we're both Nancy Drew. We'll find something—we have to." Ashley wouldn't take "No" for an answer.

"Okay, Ash. I'm down for it . . . this doing nothing is killing me."

———•———

They stood at the edge of the field where Jenny's bicycle had been found. They spontaneously reached for each other's hand as if consummating an unspoken pledge. They waded into the knee-high grass that moved like a wave on the ocean as the wind graced the rural valley.

"I swear, I feel her like her spirit is riding that wind, Ash," Danyelle said as they walked.

"Me, too."

"There's some of that police tape where they found her bike. Right there," Ashley pointed.

"I see it," Danyelle said, as she walked through the wispy grass.

"So, what are we looking for, Ash? All I see is the leftover tape," Danyelle said, staring where she imagined the bicycle had been lying.

"I don't know—there has to be a clue, something that got overlooked."

"Okay, okay. I'm looking," Danyelle said as she scanned the area.

Ashley continued to pull the grass from side to side, hoping to find something that had eluded discovery. This went on for close to an hour until Danyelle plopped down on her butt—Ashley followed Danyelle. "What are we going to do, Ash?"

"I don't know," Ashley said, beginning to lose faith.

Danyelle looked up to the sky and cried out in desperation. "Please, give us something!" As the echo of her voice trailed off and she started to stand, something caught her eye. At first, she thought it was a trick played by the afternoon light, but she looked again and saw a faint, brief glint that seemed to emanate from the branch of a tree. "Ashley . . . do you see that?"

"What . . . where are you pointing?"

"Up in that tree—there's something that reflected the sunlight," Danyelle said, still pointing.

"Come on. Let's get a closer look," Ashley said, beginning to run.

"What is it?" Danyelle asked, breathing heavily.

"I think it's one of those cameras."

"Cameras?" Danyelle repeated.

"You know, those cameras hunters use to take pictures of the animals. Dad has one," Ashley said, still looking upward.

"I don't know what you're talking about," Danyelle said, looking at Ashley.

"Dad likes to see what's roaming around in the places he hunts," Ashley answered as she looked for a way to climb the tree.

"What are you doing on my property?" a man demanded as he stepped from behind a ramshackle hedge.

Neither Danyelle nor Ashley answered. They stared at the man as he approached, mesmerized by his appearance. He was low in stature; his mixed gray-and-black hair and beard were matted and unkempt. His clothes blended in with the surroundings, and it was evident—even from a distance—that both the man and his garments longed for a good washing.

"Answer me," he grunted.

"Your property?" Danyelle asked nervously.

"You're standing on my land," he fired back in a stern voice.

"We're trying to help our friend," Ashley blurted.

"What?" he asked, thrown off by Ashley's response.

"Our friend disappeared on her way home. The police found her bike right over there," Ashley gestured.

"Oh . . . that. I don't know what happened to her. Go home," he said, with no hint of sympathy.

"Why did you say it that way?" Danyelle demanded.

"Say what what way?"

"You said 'Oh, *that*,' like you knew about it," Danyelle pushed further.

"The police came by. I couldn't help them. And I can't help you, either—so go. I don't like people on my property."

"But that thing up there . . . the camera . . . it points toward the road. Didn't the police ask you about it?" Ashley asked, determined.

"They never asked."

Ashley looked at Danyelle as if to say, *This guy is an idiot.*

"They never asked. Well, *we're* asking. Did your camera pick up anything?" Ashley asked.

He said nothing for a moment as he looked at each of the girls. "I don't want to get in the middle of this thing."

"She's our friend," Danyelle said quietly.

"Maybe, but it has nothing to do with me," he said coldly.

"Didn't you hear what Danyelle said? She's our friend. Wherever she is, I know she's scared, and she needs our help," Ashley responded in an incredulous tone. "Don't *you* have friends?"

"Don't have 'em, don't want 'em. People always let you down in the end. Now, you heard me! Get off my land."

Danyelle and Ashley again exchanged glances before Danyelle ran to the man who was walking away. She took his hand. He tried to pull his hand away, but Danyelle wouldn't let go. "Sir, I'm sorry for whatever happened to you. But our friend's name is 'Jenny,' and she hasn't let anybody down. She would do anything for anyone, and now it's our turn to help her. Please, can you help us?" Danyelle finished, her eyes welling up.

It had been years since anyone had taken his hand. He looked at Danyelle and was transported back to his eighth birthday, when he'd held his mother's hand when crossing a street on the way to Woolworth's. He hadn't thought of that day for many years, but as Danyelle held his hand, he remembered how safe he felt being with his mom, as if nothing in the world could harm him. His mother died only three months later from pancreatic cancer, and, with no father in the picture, he was shuffled off to live with his aunt and uncle, who'd never wanted children. The home was cold and unloving, and the small boy never understood why his mother had to die. Life only got tougher from there—troubled foster homes when his aunt and uncle later refused to raise him, time spent in reform school, difficult deployments in Afghanistan—culminating in an austere, lonely life.

"What do you want from me?"

"Did your camera catch anything that could help us?" Danyelle asked gently.

"Come with me," he said, as he looked again at Danyelle and then at Ashley.

Ashley and Danyelle trudged through field and forest, following a man they didn't know, fighting off the feeling they should flee, driven only by a desire to save their friend. They eventually arrived at a small mobile home that looked like it hadn't moved since the day it arrived. Its worn, unkempt exterior blended with the terrain, as if deliberately camouflaged. He held the door and waved the girls in ahead. Both Ashley and Danyelle felt like they were playing a part in a bad horror film but chose to push their fears aside and stepped over the threshold.

The inside of his home was much the same as the outside. He moved clutter from two small chairs and invited them to sit. He sat in a chair opposite, turned on the monitors, and fired up an app. In short order, he had pulled up images that the camera had captured.

"I'm sorry I came across as such an ass, and I know I don't make much of an appearance. Hell, I don't hardly know how to be with people . . . I reckon I'm more hermit than man nowadays. So let me try again: My name is Houston . . . I understand it was my grandpa's name."

"I'm Danyelle, and this is Ashley."

"Well, nice to make your acquaintance. Y'all don't know what I've been through . . . how could ya? Maybe I should have come forward sooner, but . . . well, let's just say the police don't much care for me—and the feeling's mutual. I should'a looked past that, knowin' a kid's life might be at stake. Fact is, my little camera did snag some pictures that maybe could lead somewhere. If y'all tell me where to send the images, I'll get them to ya. I know you'll need to get them to the police, but I'd appreciate it if you can keep my name out of it. Believe me, it will go better for you and me."

"We'll try," Ashley answered.

"If you get no satisfaction working with local law enforcement, let me know. Back in the war, I was in intelligence. It's been a long time, but I think some of what I learned would still work today."

"Really? Okay, thanks," Danyelle said, not knowing exactly what he meant.

Though the girls hadn't completely let down their guard, they were beginning to feel that Houston wasn't a menace—only a lonely, hurting soul who'd decided it was best to pull away from the rhythms of life to survive.

Ashley and Danyelle didn't stay long after they gave Houston their email addresses but parted on good terms.

"Y'all know where to find me if you need help," he said as he watched the girls walk away.

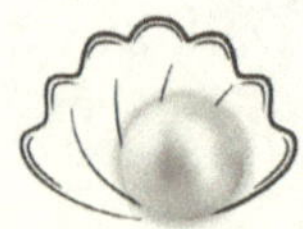

CHAPTER EIGHTEEN

JENNY LAY AWAKE, staring at the wall. Her attitude had grown bleaker with each passing day, and she could see the effect in the mirror when she dared look. She was coming to realize this may be her "new normal." Though she asked him each day when she could leave, she knew in her heart she might never see her family again. Her head ached from repeatedly considering the many scenarios her mind fabricated—each ultimately converging to one question: *Why would he ever let me leave?* Jenny knew she was his cash cow, and, if she refused to cooperate, he would make her life even more miserable. And even if his exploitation of her and the pearl ran its course, why would he hazard releasing her? A depression the likes of which she had never experienced was turning all to gray, like a cold, rainy November day whose end wasn't visible on any horizon.

"Good morning, Jenny. We have another meeting planned for today," he stated in a sickly-sweet voice.

"This is our fourth meeting. You said if I did what you asked, I could go home," were Jenny's first words.

"Just a few more appointments, and you'll be free to leave."

"So, three more?" Jenny said, trying to force him to give a definitive answer.

"Yes, yes—just a few more," he answered, skirting her question.

"Can you at least let my parents know I'm okay?" Jenny asked, anticipating she would receive a pat answer.

"I'm afraid that is impossible . . . too high a risk, but don't get all gloomy. Like I said, it won't be long until you can tell them yourself."

Jenny shook her head and changed the subject, asking a question in as sarcastic a tone as she could manage, "What is it today? Another millionaire trying to make more millions?"

"Very funny, Jenny. In a way, but this one has an interesting twist."

"How do you find these people?"

"I've made many acquaintances in my years traveling the globe. And they—or those they know—are interested in having important questions answered."

"Let's get this over with," Jenny grunted.

"Don't be in such a hurry. Our guest won't be ready for another 30 minutes or so. And, remember the rules: If you attempt to alert anyone to our 'arrangement,' I will take immediate action—meaning we will leave this location, and it will prolong your stay."

Jenny spent the 30 minutes eating the provided bowl of lukewarm oatmeal and trying to shake off her despair by reading an old *Vogue Magazine* that had fallen behind the bare corner bookshelf in her one-room "cell." The edition was from the year 1953, and the dresses, outfits, and ads amused her; she wondered what it was like to grow up in that time—anything to take her mind away from the present.

"Are you ready?"

"Like I said, let's get it over with."

"Here's your pearl," he said, as he extended his hand.

Jenny looked at the pearl for a moment before she took it from his hand and took her seat.

In short order, two men appeared onscreen. The session began with the customary niceties, which made apparent the reason for two people—one was playing the role of interpreter. After a slight hesitation, the man sitting next to the translator began to explain himself and why he was there. He had a troubled expression and spoke quietly. The translation slowed the story, but it also made it more pointed. As a young man, he'd been a true believer in the political system that governed his country. Nothing was more important than the regime, and anything that put it at risk had to be stamped out—the end justified the means. During this time, a movement started that was gaining strength. It wasn't a military crusade, but peaceful—they wanted enhanced human rights, openness, and justice for those who had been persecuted. The government secretly wished this challenge to the status quo *was* military in nature, as peaceful insurgencies were harder to manage from a public-relations perspective. After exhausting efforts to bring this young faction back to the fold by diplomatic means, the hammer was brought down in medieval fashion, killing and jailing large numbers, to the outcry of most of the world's nations.

In the years after, the practiced propaganda machine was able to effectively eliminate the event from history. During the session, the man stopped on several occasions to gain control of his emotions, which was unusual, given his current standing in the very government he described. In fact, sharing his story was extraordinary, but this man, in his elder years, was in moral crisis, for, as a young man, he was the one who followed the order to put down the peaceful revolution. He looked those young people in the eye as they were violently crushed. He was praised by his leaders, but he was never able to push those sights, sounds, and smells from his memory. After his testimony was finished, he asked his question: "Will I burn in hell for what I've done?"

With the sound of his last word hanging in the air, Jenny began to speak: "As part of your journey in the afterlife, you will be made to feel and understand the pain and suffering you caused, not only to those directly affected but also to those who knew and loved those you harmed. It will be very difficult for you, and, in a way, you could describe it as 'hell.' After this period of atonement and growth, your spirit will continue to move forward. What you also fail to understand, as do most humans, is that, in harming others, you harm yourself, as we are all born from the same source and carry a portion of it in us—we are truly sisters and brothers. In contrast, the good you do in this world, particularly for your fellow men and women, also follows you to the world beyond, in a way, *offsetting* your transgressions. So, there is yet an opportunity to affect your experience when you pass to the other side."

After Jenny's words were translated, the man spoke again. "Thank you for your direct responses. I shall do all within my power to make right what I did all those years ago." These were the last words translated for the man, whose eyes told of the pain in his heart.

CHAPTER NINETEEN

HOUSTON WAS TRUE TO HIS WORD, as both Danyelle and Ashley received the photos his camera had captured. They shared them with their parents and Jenny's mother and father. It broke their hearts to briefly see Jenny before she and the van were gone. They manipulated the images as best they could and thought they were able to discern the van's make, but they wasted little time before calling Ben and the other policemen who were investigating Jenny's disappearance. Everyone was on the call.

"Some old guy with a hunting camera," Ashley responded when asked where the photos had come from.

"If it's that Houston character, you better be careful. I don't trust that guy," the officer warned.

"Yeah, okay—but what about the photos? . . . I mean this is big . . . right?" Jenny's mom asked, finding it difficult to contain her emotions.

"I'll get this to the lab and the FBI right away. This is great information, but it's important that you remain patient," the officer said, trying to minimize their expectations before ending the call.

"I don't understand why he didn't sound more positive. This is the first piece of evidence that means anything, and it took the girls to find it," Beth argued with Seth, as if he were at fault.

"I agree, but you know how the police are . . . they have a job to do, and. . . ."

Beth didn't let Seth finish. "It sounds like you're defending them. They need to get off their asses and find her." Weeks of sleeplessness and desperation were tearing her apart. "I'm sorry," she said, after sitting in silence for the better part of fifteen minutes.

"I know, sweetheart—this is killing me, too."

——————

"They're saying it's a common white Ford van. They couldn't make out the plates, and there wasn't an angle to see the guy's face. Something else about no phone calls. I don't know—I stopped listening," Ashley repeated in a strained voice, trying to explain to Danyelle what the police were saying. "No, they said it isn't going to be easy. They're going to chase down leads, but it could be weeks."

"What are we going to do, Ash?" Danyelle asked in despair.

"I know they said not to trust him, but I think we should ask Houston. I mean, he said if we needed help . . ."

"We do need help, and I'm not sure what it means exactly, but didn't he say he was in intelligence or something?" Danyelle asked.

"Yeah, he did say that. Isn't that like spy stuff?"

"I think so. I'm down for it . . . I'll send him an email," Danyelle decided.

——— · ———

"I didn't expect to see y'all again once you talked to the boys in blue," Houston said after opening the door to his trailer.

"The police and FBI are saying it's going to take a lot of time to check out all the leads, and we're afraid for our friend," Ashley said.

"And they said y'all should come and talk to me?"

"Not exactly . . . they said we shouldn't trust you," Danyelle volunteered.

"That's more like it," Houston half-laughed. "So, what's this all about? My gut is telling me this wasn't a random thing."

The girls looked at each other but said nothing.

"Hey, they might not like me, but the FBI is pretty good. They had to ask the same question," he said, after seeing Ashley and Danyelle's hesitation.

"They did ask, but we thought if we told them the whole story, they wouldn't believe us," Ashley answered.

"Try me," Houston quietly fired back.

"I think you're going to tell us to leave afterwards, but here goes . . ." Danyelle told the story from crazy start to where it stood.

"Well, that's a new one on me," Houston said after taking some time to consider what he'd heard.

"Come on, Danyelle," Ashley said as she looked up at Houston.

"Y'all are a little too jumpy. I said, 'That's a new one.' I didn't say I didn't believe y'all," Houston began. When I was in Afghanistan, I saw some things those tribal holy men did that no one could explain away. And I've had my own, call 'em *spiritual experiences*. No, I can't stand here and judge nothin', but someone else knew about this pearl . . . .I'd bet my farm on it."

"I don't know how some kidnapper would know anything about Jenny or the pearl," Ashley said, trying to think who might have done this.

"Hey, I've seen people talk not knowin' there were ears listenin'," Houston said to help Ashley understand.

"So, you're going to help us?" Ashley replied.

"I don't know if I can, but I'm throwin' in."

"Really?" Danyelle asked in disbelief.

"So did your friend have this pearl with her?"

"For sure," Danyelle answered quickly.

"Okay, and did they tell you if any cell-phone activity was detected?"

"What did they say about the phone?" Ashley asked herself as she tapped her hands nervously on her knees. "I was so pissed they weren't telling us they were on the way to rescue Jenny. I remember them saying something about an errant text . . . like one stupid character, and that they couldn't make out the plates."

"Yeah, well, they have the best software in the world and damn good analysts, but there's some homemade stuff I play with. I know y'all think I'm an old hick, but I'm pretty good with a computer," he said with an almost imperceptible grin.

"I was playin' with the images after I sent them to y'all. I ain't sayin' this will solve the riddle, but there are a pair of things I noticed that may give us something to sink our teeth into. I'm also puzzling over that *errant text*, but that's a headache for another time. First thing, your friend was riding a bike with some old-school chrome fenders, and I picked up something in a reflection—meanin' two numbers from the van's plate. Then there's that cartop carrier. It may look like a thousand others, but it's custom, and only one outfit makes 'em . . . real high-end stuff for serious outdoorsy people. I'm thinkin' these will give us a good place to start. Let me dig a little deeper, and then we can talk about next steps," Houston finished with a small smile.

"Houston, we don't know what to say. I mean, we're losing hope . . . thank you so much," Danyelle smiled in return.

"Now y'all can't lose hope. I've been in some tough scrapes, and I made it through. There ain't no guarantees, but I think whoever has Jenny needs her alive *and* that pearl."

Upon leaving, each of the girls hugged the gray-bearded man who smelled of hay and garden soil. The girls' gesture of endearment touched Houston as, by his own choice, it had been years since he'd known any human kindness. An old feeling was rising in his heart—the feeling of making a difference; to his surprise, it made him happy.

"Y'all keep an eye on your email . . . I'll be writing soon," Houston said as he waved goodbye.

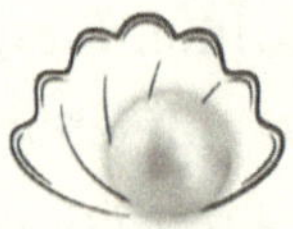

CHAPTER TWENTY

JENNY LOOKED DOWN AT HER ARMS. What she saw further impacted her mental state. Her once-toned and defined muscle was fading. She made an effort to consume the food she was provided, but it seemed it did little to sustain her. Even her unsympathetic captor was concerned. "You need to eat more," he said, as he placed her breakfast tray on the table.

"I need to go home. I need to be back with my family."

"I'm glad you mentioned that because *I've* been thinking about family. *We're* a family, aren't we? You're like a daughter to me, after all. If you give me a chance, I think you could be very happy. Let's face it, in a few years, you'll be either leaving for university or moving to a place of your own. So, this is a natural progression."

Were it not for her caring nature and her diminished state, his twisted suggestion and warped logic would have driven her to rise and face him with all the fight she had left. Instead, she chose to turn her eyes toward a stark-white wall opposite where she sat. The bland surface was, in a way, an analog to her once-vibrant irises that were now dull. Her deepest fears were now solidified—that she would never see her family and friends again.

"Give it some thought. It could be a wonderful adventure . . . we make a good team, or should I say *family*," he offered as he left the room.

Her focus-less gaze continued even after she heard the lock secure the door.

CHAPTER TWENTY-ONE

HOUSTON'S EMAIL REQUESTED that they meet again.

"This grizzly old vet made a few phone calls. Y'all remember me talkin' about that cartop carrier?" He continued after the girls nodded. "Turns out that outfit keeps good records, and those records show they installed one of their custom jobs on a white Ford van of the same vintage we're lookin' for. And wouldn't you know it—they record license-plate numbers . . . it's tied to their lifetime warranty."

"So, you know who the kidnapper is?" Danyelle asked excitedly.

"Not yet, we don't. The plate number in their books sure enough contained the numbers I saw, but just 'cause this looks like the van, it doesn't mean the owner was in on it. But this led to my next step. I searched public records and figured out who the current owner is and where he calls home. He is a Mr. Samson and lives some forty miles from here."

"Let's go . . . like *now*!" Ashley barked as she jumped to her feet.

"You'd best sit back down, Miss Ashley. This needs to be managed the right way, or it might blow up and not lead to Jenny."

"I don't understand. Don't you think he has Jenny?" Ashley asked, her hope beginning to wane as she sat back down.

"Maybe, but we gotta think this through. What if the creep who grabbed her 'borrowed' the van? If we start askin' all kind of questions, this Samson guy might tip off the bastard who has Jenny, and he'll make a run for it—*with Jenny*. Look, whoever took your friend is smart. He picked a spot where he thought no one was looking. I, for sure, think he knew about this pearl. I'm also thinkin' that *errant text* was a ping to let the kidnapper know she was going to ride her bike home. And with a girl in tow, he vanished, and, so far, he's evaded some of the best law enforcement in the world. Girls, we don't want to screw this up now."

"So, what do we do, Houston? We've got to find her," Danyelle pleaded.

"I can't believe I'm sayin' this, but I'm thinkin' it's time to meet with the boys in blue."

"You mean you want us to tell them all this stuff?" Ashley asked with obvious worry.

"No, I mean it's time for *me* to eat some humble pie and go with you."

"No lie?" Ashley asked, knowing how hard this would be for Houston.

"No lie," Houston responded.

Though they didn't want to, the girls elected to keep this knowledge to themselves until they met with the police. There had been so many false alarms, and they knew an audience was the last thing Houston needed.

"You . . . what is he doing here?" Ben asked when Houston, Danyelle, and Ashley entered the station.

"He's with us," Ashley volunteered.

"I told you to stay clear of him."

"Look, I know I've been a pain in your ass, Ben, but I ain't here to cause any trouble. These kids are trying to find their friend, and we have something you need to see," Houston said, respectfully.

Ben stared at Houston, trying to determine if there was any truth in his words, as if he were a suspect at an interrogation. "If this is a hoax, I will personally see to it you are locked up—I'll make up a charge if I have to. These kids have been through it."

"I can't blame ya, Ben, but I'm here 'cause I want to see that Ashley and Danyelle are reunited with their friend. Look, I don't like talkin' about it, but I was held captive by some Afghani bad guys during the war, and it was almost the end of me. It's how I lost these two fingers." Houston raised his right hand so Ben could see. "I know what it means to be held against your will. We've got to find her."

"Houston!" Ashley shrieked, horrified—and at the same time *shocked*—that she hadn't noticed.

Danyelle was unable to utter a word but stood wide-eyed, wondering what terrible things Houston had endured.

"Good Lord, Houston, why didn't you tell me this before? It would have helped me understand what was going on—with *you* I mean," Ben said, shaking his head as he thought about their previous encounters.

"Like I said, I don't care much for talkin' about it."

Houston refused to dwell any further on his captivity and instead laid out all he had discovered, complete with a log of the steps he had taken to date and the enhanced photographs from his hunting camera.

"Houston, this is some good work—really good work," Ben said in earnest after the presentation. "If you were in my seat, what would you do next?"

"I would like to lay eyes on this Samson's phone records—cell, home, everything. I'd like to know his location shortly before Jenny disappeared. And I'd like to see what hit his bank account over the last few months," Houston answered, not expecting he would be granted anything on his list.

"That will require warrants. And I think we—meaning you and I—need to show all this to the FBI; they can help with the warrants," Ben fired back without hesitation.

"So much for stayin' out of this," Houston chuckled. "I don't think the FBI will be all that keen on me being part of this."

"You won't be on your own, Houston. The hell with the past—and I'll tell the FBI the same. This could save a kid's life," Ben said, extending his hand.

Houston looked at Ben's outstretched hand. "We can't tip this Samson off," Houston said as he shook Ben's hand.

"10–4 on that, Houston. We'll have to be careful," Ben acknowledged.

Danyelle and Ashley were amazed that the men who were standing before them were now willing to work as a team. A short time ago, Houston wanted nothing to do with them *or* Jenny, and now he was leading the charge to save her. Positive developments had been rare since Jenny disappeared, but observing these men joining their efforts triggered a feeling of hope that was rising in Danyelle and Ashley's hearts.

CHAPTER TWENTY-TWO

"I THINK WE'VE STAYED IN ONE PLACE long enough . . . don't you think so, sweetheart?" he asked as if he had a hundred times before.

"*Sweetheart*?" Jenny asked as she turned her head, not sure if she'd heard him correctly.

"Perhaps a little too soon," he replied nonchalantly.

"*A little too soon*?" Jenny asked, more forcefully this time.

"Yes, I haven't given you enough time to get used to being a family. Wouldn't a father call his daughter 'sweetheart'?"

"I will never be your *daughter* . . . never!" Jenny answered with palpable hatred.

"Like I said, a bit too soon," he answered, thrown back by Jenny's intensity. Let's knock out today's appointment and then talk about next steps."

"What *next steps*?"

"We've been here long enough. We need to find new lodging . . . somewhere beautiful . . . somewhere exotic. I can afford it now."

"I want to go home!" Jenny said so loudly that he closed the door to the room.

"It won't do you any good to yell. This room is soundproof and well-concealed. Besides, I'm sick of that tired old, 'I want to go home' theme. We need to learn to make a home together . . . I've told you this."

A single tear ran down Jenny's cheek as she fell back into the chair from which she had just stood. Spending her life with a parasite was more than she bargained for. At that moment, from somewhere deep in her mind, the thought of ending her life arose, and it frightened her.

CHAPTER TWENTY-THREE

"THE WARRANTS WERE EXECUTED early this morning. Your Samson didn't see it coming, and he started talking as soon as they picked him up. He lent his van to this college professor. This schoolteacher paid Samson $4,500 for the use of his van and for that single-character text as an alert. The FBI and other groups of law enforcement are on their way to visit this academic—warrants in hand," Ben informed Houston, Ashley, and Danyelle, whom he had called to the station. By this point, all the families had been informed.

"Take us there," Ashley demanded.

"I assumed you would ask. I'm permitted to take you, as long as you promise to stay well back. If any of you make one move without my permission, I will personally cuff you and put you in the rear of my vehicle. Is that understood?" Ben asked in his official cop voice.

Houston nodded, and Ashley and Danyelle agreed.

"I don't understand. Why are you here?"

"We have probable cause that you may be involved in a kidnapping, and we have a warrant to search your residence," Special Agent in Charge Jim Jackson said as he handed the professor the paperwork.

"Have you lost your mind? Do you know who I am? I'm a professor at a prestigious university. I merely need to make one call and . . . "

Jim cut him off. "Feel free to make any calls you need to, sir."

The house was searched from stem to stern, with no sign of Jenny.

Danyelle and Ashley could faintly hear the officers saying they would have to pull out. Their body language spoke to their disappointment. Danyelle and Ashley began to walk, not knowing what else to do to rid themselves of the discouragement and heartbreak—where was Jenny if not here? As the bevy of law-enforcement vehicles slowly pulled away, Danyelle and Ashley mindlessly turned down a side road that skirted the professor's property. A garbage truck was pulling to the side to pick up a line of bags, which, upon first observation, belonged to the neighbor. The girls stopped to give the crew room to do their work. Ashley happened to peer into the throat of the compactor that was beginning to tear open the green plastic sacks.

"*Stop!*" Ashley shouted so loudly that the truck's driver instinctively raised the heavy mechanical jaw and turned off the ignition.

Jim and a marshal who'd remained behind talking to Ben turned to look as well.

"What's wrong? I thought I ran over someone," the driver growled, aggravated with Ashley.

"What house did those bags come from?" Ashley asked, ignoring the driver's attitude.

"Which bags? Why does it matter?" he asked, more annoyed this time.

"Please, do you know which house those green bags came from?" Ashley asked in a tone that begged for some understanding, some sympathy.

The man at the rear of the truck spoke up. From over there, where that stuck-up guy lives. He always uses the green heavy-duty bags. Come to think of it, he put them three houses down the road. I didn't think about it until now."

By this time, Ben and the two remaining officers were standing beside Ashley and Danyelle. "What's the problem?"

"Does that professor have a wife or daughter?" Ashley asked Jim.

Jim wasn't sure where Ashley was going with this line of questioning, but he played along. "Why do you ask?"

Ashley pointed at the green bag whose side had split after being partially crushed. There, the remnants of a box of sanitary napkins was hanging.

"We looked for his trash but found next to nothing. You say he moved his bags down the street?" Jim quizzed the trashman.

"Yeah, they usually sit right there, but this time, they were down by the yellow house," he said as he pointed.

Jim pulled out his phone. "I want everyone back here. I know and I don't give a damn how inconvenient. Get everyone to turn around and come back to the suspect's house."

"So, can we get on down the road? There's like fifty houses to go," the driver pressed.

"You go nowhere until I say. If I have to, I'll impound your truck."

"What's so special about some woman throwing away her girl stuff?" the man at the rear mumbled as he walked around the side of the truck.

———

"You're basing this on a box of tampons?" one of the marshals asked. Maybe his girlfriend stayed over."

"He said he lived alone, and what woman would have that guy, anyway? Didn't you tell me you broke a case based on a fishing lure?"

"That was different. The guy claimed to be casting for bass using . . ."

"Spare me the detail," Jim interrupted.

"Okay, but if this thing hinges on a feminine-hygiene product, you're writing it up," the marshal responded with a grin that was barely perceptible.

"Look, if he's got the kid hidden away in some dungeon, we'd never forgive ourselves. This time, I want you tapping on walls, on floors, on ceilings. I'm convinced there's an entry to a well-hidden room, probably something underground. If anything gives you the slightest pause, call me, and we'll dig into it. There's something about this guy that's not right."

"I won't stand for this!" the professor all but yelled when he answered the door.

"I'm sorry, sir, but further information has become available, and there are a few follow-up things we must investigate."

"I've already been in contact with my attorney, and I assure you someone will lose their job over this," the professor threatened further.

"I understand, sir. That is your right. Now, please stand aside."

The frustrated law-enforcement team did what they were told. They searched high and low, tapping, pounding, knocking, and showed nothing for it.

"Look, Jim, this isn't panning out. I don't like the guy, either; I think he's an ass, but I don't think he has the girl."

Jim nodded and slowly walked across the kitchen as he took a long draw from the water bottle he was carrying. As he crossed in front of the pantry door, a deputy, who had been examining the food closet emerged, and the two collided. The bottle fell to the floor and rolled inside the pantry, all but emptying the bottle.

"Sorry, sir. I didn't see you," the young deputy said apologetically. "I'll get something to mop it up."

"I'll clean it up . . . clumsy fool," the professor chided.

"Sir," the deputy said in the inflection of a question. "Look—look there."

The agent turned his head to see where the deputy was pointing. The water that had spilled was flowing quickly under the pantry's baseboard, not pooling, almost as if it were swirling down a drain.

"Get out of my way so I can clean up this mess," the professor snapped as he tried to enter the small space.

"Hold him back," Jim said, as he studied the water's behavior. He probed the wall and noted that the shelves weren't continuous and that the cans and cartons stored on the shelves were closely packed together—except where the shelving was butted. There the stored provisions were separated by roughly an inch from the lowest shelf to the highest. Then he found it—a concealed latch, which he pulled. A door-like section swung open a few inches.

"Hold onto him . . . I don't want him to budge one millimeter," the agent said to the deputy standing beside the professor.

Jim fully opened the panel, revealing a narrow, descending staircase. Not knowing what he might encounter, he pulled his Glock from its holster before embarking. With only the light from the pantry behind, he carefully moved down the gloomy passage. As if tired from bearing the load, the boards groaned with each successive step. He let his eyes adjust to the dimly lighted space until he could see a heavily padded door immediately ahead. Two metal bolts, one high and one low, made clear the intent—make escape impossible. With weapon still in hand, he fought the lower one first. Despite his attempt to quietly slide the pin, his effort was for naught, as it unexpectedly released and made a snapping noise that briefly echoed before being absorbed by the soundproofing that covered all the surrounding surfaces.

Jim looked up the stairway and shook his head. He regripped the handgun in his sweaty palm before reaching for the upper latch. It, too, resisted movement until he gently leaned against the door, which took the pressure off the steel fastener, allowing it to easily slide. Not knowing what he might encounter, he stood away from the face of the door as he prepared to pull it open. With no further hesitation, he jerked it open and, in a quick series of fluid motions, scanned the room, stepping into the stark space, now with two hands on his firearm. When he was sure that there was no immediate threat, he slightly lowered his piece and proceeded forward, toward the bedding lying on the floor on the far side of the room. "Jenny?" he gently questioned. When the blanketed figure didn't move, he once again raised the handgun. "Jenny?" he spoke more demonstrably.

"What do you want?" Jenny asked quietly, not recognizing the different voice tone.

"I'm Jim, a Special Agent of the FBI. Is that you, Jenny?"

Jenny slowly turned her head and opened her eyes. "What?" she asked, not yet understanding the situation.

"Jenny . . . I'm here to help you . . . I'm from the FBI. He can't hurt you anymore."

She raised upward and squinted trying to focus. "FBI?"

"What's your name?" he asked trying to get her to think.

"I'm Jenny," she answered.

"I know," he smiled. Can you stand?" he asked as he slowly closed the distance between them.

"I think so," she answered, now weak from poor diet and her debilitating confinement.

She uncovered herself and prepared to stand.

Now convinced there was no hidden danger, Jim holstered his gun and carefully helped Jenny to her feet. "We have some EMTs here who can help you."

"How did you find me?"

"I wish we could claim credit for it, but it was your friends and a crazy old coot named Houston," he said and smiled as he put his arm around her.

"Danyelle and Ash?"

"Yes, and Houston."

"I don't think I know Houston," she said, as they walked toward the open door.

"You'll meet him later."

Jenny had suffered substantial weight loss and stumbled as she walked. Jim lifted her like a bushel of apples, carrying her up the stairs and through the pantry.

"Tell them how well I treated you, Jenny . . . she's like a daughter to me," the professor pled as Jim emerged with Jenny.

"Where's my pearl?" Jenny mumbled when she heard his voice.

"Your pearl?" Jim asked, not understanding.

"Here it is, Jenny," Iman said as he removed the orb from his pocket, still covered in her grandmother's handkerchief, and handed it to her. Tell them we're friends, Jenny."

"Cuff him, and get him out of here," Jim said, fighting an urge to thump the man, "and call her parents."

"They're on the way," another agent nodded.

The sunshine warmed Jenny's face, and, as she breathed the fresh air, she felt an energy rise in her heart. "Can I try walking?"

"Are you sure?"

"Yeah, but stay close, please," she smiled.

When Danyelle and Ashley saw her stand, they ran to her, calling her name. They put their arms around her to support her as they had supported each other since meeting in summer camp, which, as they stood here now, seemed a lifetime ago.

"I never thought I would see you again," Jenny said, as she looked at their tear-streaked faces. "How did you find me?"

"You got three days to talk about it?" Ashley laughed as she repositioned to take more of Jenny's weight.

Danyelle and Jenny joined Ashley in laughter.

Jenny woke just as the sun was rising over the blue-green ocean. Several months had passed, and she was now looking over the same beach where it all began. She was struggling with anxiety, panic attacks, anger, and trust issues. Despite this, she was determined to live without fear and decided to take an early-morning walk on the sand. The further she traveled, the more the voice in her head shouted at her to be careful, not to venture too far, to watch who was near. She hated this voice and fought back by trying to change to a positive line of thought, as her therapist had encouraged, but she wondered if she could ever rid herself of the repressive negativity. Jenny arrived at a pier that extended well away from the shore, and she decided to walk the weathered planks to the pier's end.

As she stood staring at the vast, open waters of the Atlantic, she recalled tales she had read in volumes that described villains who, to her, never seemed real, but now she'd come face to face with real treachery, and it deeply saddened her. She contemplated her future and wondered if it had been ruined; she didn't know if she could ever fully trust again. As these thoughts continued to prey on her mind, she rolled the pearl in her hand, which revived the memory of the day she first came to possess it—that innocent day seemed a century in the past. Though she had disclosed it to no one, she had resolved to cast the pearl back into the sea, and this seemed as good a time as any. She raised her arm and was ready to discard the gold sphere, when a murky figure began to take shape just to the left of where she stood. Initially, it frightened her, and made her think she might be on the verge of madness, but, surprisingly, the fear began to subside, and, in its place, a peace began to take hold.

Like trying to see an object in the dark, she focused her gaze to the side to see if it would clarify what was taking shape. This did little to help, and, instead, she was drawn to look more intently, like a nocturnal insect that circles a light in the black of night. It reminded her of an article she'd read about what happens in a butterfly's cocoon during its mystical metamorphosis—its original shape replaced and replaced and replaced, until its final, exquisite form is realized. All the while, without the aid of her ears, in her mind, she could hear the faint sound of children laughing during play, of adults telling tales of younger days, of a childhood song that lifted her heart, of the early morning symphony of birds singing, of a lion roaring, of a horse's neigh . . . just like the figure that was changing and forming, the sounds were varied and numerous, but all were somehow pleasing.

At the culmination of this transformation stood a man dressed like a beach bum—raggedy shorts, old T-shirt bearing the name of a local high school, and well-worn sandals. His long, gray beard and equally long, gray hair moved easily in the steady breeze. Jenny couldn't make sense of what she had seen and had the sensation of not knowing how long she had been standing on the wooden surface. She didn't know what to say or even if she should speak.

"You've had a time of it, haven't you?" the man asked in a voice that was reminiscent of another she'd heard, though she couldn't bring it to the fore in her mind.

"I guess I have," Jenny answered, surprised by his question.

"I'm sorry," he responded, with a gentle smile.

"Your voice—it's so familiar, but I can't quite . . ." Jenny said as she struggled to remember.

"My appearance was somewhat different when last we met," he said, still wearing a calm, easy smile.

She stared at him intently. "*The oyster!*" Jenny exclaimed.

"Very good, Jenny," he answered.

"You're a person?" Jenny asked.

"More spirit than person, but having pulled the talking-oyster move on you, I thought it only fair to appear as human," he said and laughed.

"I know you're trying to cheer me up, but I don't feel much like laughing," Jenny said glumly.

"People can be extremely cruel, and I'm sorry you had to endure all that pain," he said so earnestly she felt it resonate.

"I feel like that sicko user ruined my life," her anger apparent. "I was trying to help people, to be kind, and look what happened. I'm sure the next thing will be for some hater to say I'm evil and that the pearl is, too. I mean—what is *wrong* with people?"

"The man who held you captive was an insecure soul who, from his earliest days was never loved the way he should have been. So, in his desperation, he looked for affirmation from others. He thought that praise from his colleagues and the trappings that would accompany his "discovery" would validate his existence—that he did have value. That doesn't excuse his behavior. Many, many, people don't feel loved or love themselves because of past hurts and rejections by parents or friends or partners, but they don't do what this man did. As far as people misunderstanding the nature of the pearl and your role: I would say that most humans find it difficult to be truly open-minded. They all like to think they are, but when they are afraid, they struggle to make sense of things," he said as he turned to face her.

"Afraid . . . what is there to be *afraid* of?"

"People are raised with certain concepts of good and evil—there are variations, but most are similar. When someone or something comes along that doesn't fit what they've been taught, even if it is good, they fear it. And when people are afraid and don't understand, rational thought takes a back seat. The next step is to find others who are similarly afraid, and, before you know it, you have a mob, and, when that happens, people will do things they would never, never, otherwise do. It's unfortunate, and human history is littered with stories of misunderstood Good Samaritans. But then, to sympathize, for just a moment, with those who are afraid, sometimes those with evil intent pose as Good Samaritans . . . life is a tricky business."

"So, there's nothing we can rely on in life . . . nothing I can rely on?" Jenny asked in frustration.

"Ah, Jenny. As hard as it is, if life were different, it wouldn't be life at all. We would be robots walking through a world with no true choice. I know this helps little, given what you've been through."

"I know—free will. I've heard that my whole life, and it's probably a good thing, but I'm tired of mean people," Jenny grunted.

Nothing was said for a few moments, and then he offered something further. "Do you know how you answered the question James asked?"

"He asked if there was a God, but I don't remember the answer. I mean, my friends tell me the basics, but not the whole answer. Why?" Jenny asked in return.

"In answering his question, you talked about an incredible loving force, a force that is in all of us and in all things. That force is something you can rely on, as it will never diminish."

"I know you mean well, Mr. Oyster, or whatever your name is, but I'm not feeling a lot of love right now. I want to get rid of this pearl and hide for the rest of my life," Jenny said as she turned to face the sea.

"I understand, and the decision is yours to make. Whatever you choose, all will be well. Let me say just a few more words before I go. I'm certain you've heard the phrase, 'That which doesn't kill you makes you stronger.' I think it should be amended in such a fashion as to convey *that which doesn't kill you and which you don't allow to poison your soul will, indeed, make you stronger.* Too many who inhabit this world carry with them scars that have only partially healed. To be sure, recovering from harm is no mean feat, but letting a wound take up permanent residence robs us of our rightful future, our calling, our reason for being. You must guard against this, Jenny. You must take the pain you hold in your breast and transform it into a force for good—not only for you but for the good of others. If you can't do this, it is much more difficult to achieve what you were born to."

"I don't know if I can," Jenny said, afraid of what the future held.

"You will, Jenny; your family and your amazing friends will help you. And don't forget what I told you when I offered the pearl . . . you have a good heart . . . an amazing heart."

Jenny managed a small smile.

"It is time for me to say goodbye, Jenny," he said, extending his hand.

She cautiously extended her hand, and, when her hand met his, the world in which she thought she was standing was no more. All began to shimmer with a light like she had never seen. It connected everything and flowed through her. As it did, her anger, her fear, her frustration, and her pain quickly faded. She felt a peace, a love, unlike any she had ever experienced. Time evaporated, and she had the elusive sense she had been here before—as if being welcomed home. She suddenly understood that evil was just an aberration, a cool current that brushes your legs in a vast, warm ocean and then is gone. With that thought, the world she knew returned, leaving her with a pressing sadness that felt like she was saying goodbye to a loved one who was boarding a train. Her eyes welled, and she wrapped her arms around her visitor, knowing he couldn't stay.

"You see, my young one, you can always rely on love," was his last statement, and then he vanished as mysteriously as he had appeared.

"Jenny, are you okay?" Danyelle cried as she and Ashley ran the dock's length to meet her.

"I think so."

"You had a weird look," Ashley said. "I mean, weirder than *normal.*"

"Geez, Ashley!" Danyelle scolded.

"So, if I wasn't messing with her, she would think something was wrong," Ashley laughed.

"You sure you're okay?" Danyelle asked with some hesitation.

"I'm okay," she answered as she reached for her friends. "I'd be lost without you guys."

"Did you toss the pearl?" Danyelle asked, wondering if that accounted for the distance in Jenny's expression.

"I was going to, but something happened to change my mind."

"Something?" Danyelle asked, almost rhetorically.

"I can't really explain it, except to say that my old oyster friend helped me see another side of things."

"*Say what?*" Ashley asked.

"It's crazy," Jenny answered as they began walking back toward the beach. "I'll tell you about it later."

"Deal! Last one there," Ashley yelled as she pulled away and began running, like she always had when they were younger.

CHAPTER TWENTY-FOUR

"ANOTHER PIECE?" Jenny asked Houston. There's plenty left."

"Y'all are going to make me fat," Houston said.

"Going to?" Ashley laughed, implying he might already qualify.

"Hey, now—I'll have y'all know that I've shed eight pounds since I started riding with Jenny."

"Just ignore her . . . that's what we do," Jenny laughed as she placed another piece of her lemon cake on his plate.

ABOUT THE AUTHOR

MICHAEL BOGGINS is the author of *Antiquity* and *Gift Of The Golden Pearl*. He lives just a stone's throw away from the mountains of western Virginia. As for his inspiration for writing, he likes to say he gathers such from the author of all things.